Praise for Retail Reality

"Authentic, humorous and inspiring real-life stories ... *Retail Reality* shows Pat's compassion and heart for helping people. It's much more than a book about shopping and style. This is a must-read to remind us that we often have an opportunity to encourage others throughout our everyday work."

~Patti Gillespie, copyeditor of *Risen Magazine* and author of *The Bottom Line: A Biography of Marvin L. "Buzz" Oates*

"Having worked in retail for many years, *Retail Reality* shines a much-needed spotlight on the industry. Pat delivers a shopping experience that is inviting, genuine, and compassionate. She is a gem in the 'retail reality' world, and her adventures will leave you wanting more."

~Jana Maloney, event planner

"*Retail Reality* is a collection of charming and delightful stories that are sure to warm your heart and touch your soul. Bravo to Pat for sharing her inspirational experiences with us."

~Monica Lynne Foster, author of the *Chanelle Series Novels*

"Pat's client stories are truly heartwarming. Her compassionate and empowering style make *Retail Reality* an inspiring read. Pat finds true meaning in her work as she shares her unique customer service that takes ordinary retail shopping and transforms it into a personable, unforgettable experience."

~Nancy Hovde, wellness consultant and author of *Uber Empowerment Quotes: 500 Inspirational Quotes for Knowledge, Insight & Wisdom*

"*Retail Reality* is a timely debut of short stories that go beyond the sales counter and touch the heart. Delightfully written, I couldn't get enough of the emotionally charged life situations. This is a treasure you will want to share with family and friends. Everyone is going to be talking about *Retail Reality*!"

~Judy Sondergard, retired interior designer and owner of JS Carpets and Interiors

Retail Reality

ADVENTURES
OF A CLOTHING STYLIST

Pat Dodge

iUniverse®

To Ann
We go back a long
way and this is what
I've been doing ~ so.....
hope you enjoy my adventures
With Love
Pat Dodge
xxoo

RETAIL REALITY
ADVENTURES OF A CLOTHING STYLIST

This is a work of fiction. All of the characters, names, incidents, organizations, and dialogue in this novel are either the products of the author's imagination or are used fictitiously.

iUniverse books may be ordered through booksellers or by contacting:

iUniverse
1663 Liberty Drive
Bloomington, IN 47403
www.iuniverse.com
1-800-Authors (1-800-288-4677)

Because of the dynamic nature of the Internet, any web addresses or links contained in this book may have changed since publication and may no longer be valid. The views expressed in this work are solely those of the author and do not necessarily reflect the views of the publisher, and the publisher hereby disclaims any responsibility for them.

Any people depicted in stock imagery provided by Thinkstock are models, and such images are being used for illustrative purposes only.
Certain stock imagery © Thinkstock.

ISBN: 978-1-5320-1832-9 (sc)
ISBN: 978-1-5320-1831-2 (e)

Library of Congress Control Number: 2017906888

Print information available on the last page.

iUniverse rev. date: 06/14/2017

*For my best friend, Terri Carlsted, who rejected every reason
I proposed as to why I couldn't write this book and gave me
the one reason why I should: "It's part of your destiny!"*

and

*In loving memory of my mama, Marta Gloria
Aranda, who left my side on June 13, 2015.*

Contents

Stories in *Retail Reality*
are inspired by real-life events.

Acknowledgments

I have learned in life that no one accomplishes anything on his or her own. Nothing compares to the loving support of individuals who want to empower you and see you succeed. With that said, I would like to take this opportunity to recognize and thank those who supported me on this incredible journey of becoming an author.

On January 22, 2013, my best friend, Terri Carlsted, came to my home and said, "I'm here with a message. It's time for you to start writing your book." She spoke with such intensity and wisdom that there was nothing I could say to refute her words. And believe me—I tried! Best friends have a way of making you do things that no one else can. I never would have undertaken this project had it not been for her belief in me and my stories. These "adventures" went from being in my journals to becoming a book. Thank you so much for your loving persistence, "O"!

My friend Rich Scopelli played numerous roles on this journey. His professional background as a therapist provided insights into behaviors, which allowed me to understand and develop my story lines. As a friend, he always listened to me and encouraged me when I felt I couldn't go on, especially when my mama was dying. I will always be appreciative of his kindness and generosity in allowing me to visit the serenity of his lake home. He has enriched my life by being a genuine, loving, and caring friend.

One day, my customer Kathleen Fenton asked what I had been up to. I responded that I was in the process of writing a book. Kathleen was quite surprised and explained that perhaps she could offer a professional viewpoint. She read some of my stories and, days later, offered to be an editorial adviser. I gained not only an adviser but also the friendship of someone whom I have come to love and respect immensely. Dearest, for your generosity of time, wisdom, and kindness, I am forever grateful.

My daughter Candace and son-in-law, Jonathan, live two thousand miles away. However, despite the distance and their own busy lives, they were always available to offer substantial and meaningful suggestions, as well as loving encouragement.

My son, Jordan, and his wife, Jocelyn, likewise provided insights and suggestions for which I was appreciative.

My daughter Amy consistently provided loving support by expressing pride in my efforts and encouragement that I was on the right track. Trust me when I say she was patient and invaluable in helping me sharpen my computer skills. I couldn't have done it without her!

Lauren Meyer was also instrumental in the development of this book. Months after her mom, my best friend, Terri, challenged me to write a book, I invited both of them to read and discuss the potential of twelve stories I had written. Lauren, who is a talented writer, said point-blank, "These are book-worthy." It still brings tears to my eyes to recall that moment. My Lauren, you will reap what you have sown—blessings!

My sister, Marta Meek, generously provided financial and emotional support in bringing this book to life. It's wonderful to be reunited and rejoice together. Mama is smiling down upon us.

Through the years, I have been extremely fortunate to have worked with a number of talented and successful individuals. Their generosity of wisdom, time, commitment, kindness, and encouragement has impacted me on various levels. I strive to honor their efforts in my life by being my best and emulating their talent whenever possible. With deepest appreciation and thanks, I wish to acknowledge Brandon Stuart, Aram Beloian, Farhang Milani, Sara Stiles, Lawrence Pineda, Daniel Craft, Misty Moshier, Michael Corum, Julie Grupe, Heidi Ryan, Krista Gonzalez, Tracy Balogh, Greg Bazarnik, Juliet Hamman, Sofia Earls, Macie Avery, and Jacque Kennedy.

There is one name in particular missing from that list. He requires special attention! Years ago, I had a manager by the name of Jonathan Davis, and his impact upon my life was profound. At the time he became my manager, I was facing life changes and was deeply conflicted as to how my style of customer service fit in where I was working. Jonathan was direct in his advice and sympathetic to my struggle. He turned my frustrations around and validated my passion for always wanting to put my customers first.

"Keep doing that," he said. "Do anything and offer everything you can for the sole purpose of taking care of your customers. One day, everyone is going to catch up and understand the value of your customer service. Don't conform. Just be you! Those who don't understand will figure it out in time, but ultimately, you will be ahead of the game."

His words were energizing, and I never looked back. He gave me the freedom to be myself. Every day, my customers were my priority, and that gave me immense joy in my work. It's no wonder that many of the stories in this book took place when Jonathan was my manager. I sincerely hope he takes pride when reading this book and in knowing what his leadership instilled in my life.

Over the years, I have had the privilege of working with numerous counter partners. Many of them are my extended family, and I love them dearly. Kitty, Ramona, Laurie, Melissa, Lindy, Susan, Elaine, Jessa, Arin, Michelle, Jannette, Alexis, Jamela, Tanya, Sonam, Darrian, Nicki, Dorothy, Lauren, and Amanda, your individual and collective work ethic has permitted me to be my best. I could not do what I do without you. Thank you so much.

Kathi Aguiar and Cheryl Piazza, thank you for being my watchful eyes and helping me with the final touches on this book. Your help was invaluable.

To my customers Patricia and Jordana, thank you for helping me discover the title for this book. Retail reality, indeed! I will never forget that moment—*ever*!

To my customers Tony and Linda, thank you for your unwavering encouragement, love, and kindness.

To Donovan Garrison of dMg photos, thank you for making our photo shoot so fun and easy. You're amazing!

To Karen Phillips, thank you for your brilliant touch on my book cover. It's perfect!

I wish to thank the generosity of authors Patti Gillespie, Nancy Hovde, Cindy Sample, and Monica Lynne Foster, who assisted and encouraged me on my writing journey.

Thanks also to my AP English teacher, Bruce Grantham, who would hand me back my papers and say, "Give me more." At the time, I thought he was trying to torment me, but as I wrote this book, his words echoed. Thanks, Mr. G! I was listening!

To my wonderful, delightful customers, who provide me with the daily motivation to get up and go to work, just knowing you will be there every day with smiling faces and kind words gives me such joy and satisfaction. Thank you for your friendship and support through the years. I hope you will all enjoy reading about the reality of my work.

In closing, I thank God for His presence and favor upon my life. I've bloomed and found joy where You planted me!

With love,
Pat

Introduction

Growing up, my family members were all self-employed in some type of customer-oriented business. I remember watching my grandmother, uncles, and aunts assist not only the satisfied customer but the angry one as well. As a little girl, I would become frightened and hide as I listened to the loud and bitter words of the disgruntled customer. Minutes would pass, and my fear would turn into fascination and admiration, as my family member would diplomatically resolve the issue to everyone's satisfaction. My family clearly understood that their success depended not only on wise business strategies but also on the recognition that every customer was an invaluable asset. Back then, I had no idea that I was learning social and business skills, which would greatly influence my life.

I was raised in the San Francisco Bay Area, where my passion for the fashion industry began to evolve when I was a teenager. Anything and everything having to do with fashion captivated me because it was creative, vast, and constantly changing. I loved it all!

I would take bimonthly bus trips with my girlfriend to San Francisco, where I absorbed the latest that department stores and little boutiques had to offer. Periodicals such as *Glamour*, *Vogue*, and *W* were also invaluable tools, which helped widen my creative eye.

Today, many years later, I am a clothing stylist for a major department store in Northern California. In my work, no day is ever the same. The exciting mix of the latest styles, creative displays, and new faces keeps things fresh and moving.

I wrote *Retail Reality: Adventures of a Clothing Stylist* to give you an intimate glimpse into my day. Interestingly, when I was writing this book and mentioned it to people, they would almost always assume that it dealt with the horrors of working in a career that is considered by many to be menial. However, that assumption could not be further from the truth. Within these pages, I hope to convey that fulfillment in this profession comes from creative passion, an adherence to the highest ideals of service, and genuine regard for my customers.

As you will discover, I am often faced with complex situations that require social sensitivity, moral fiber, and on-the-spot ingenuity. I laugh, cry, cheer, get annoyed, and scratch my head and wonder, as I believe you will, when you read these stories.

I invite you now to join me in *my* world of "retail reality."

Does It Fit?
Getting It Just Right

You remember Goldilocks, the wandering girl who broke into the Bears' house and tried everything until she got it "just right." Granted, in her quest for what worked, she left a messy trail of mishaps, but you have to give her credit; she never settled!

When it comes to clothing, fit matters! You can have a beautiful garment, but if it doesn't lie properly on your body, you do yourself a disservice by wearing it anyway. The issue of proper fit is a complicated one. It's not uncommon for a woman who can't find her size on a rack to tell me she likes the garment so much she will buy it even though it doesn't fit! I'm not one to argue with customers, but on numerous occasions when I've seen that "I'm settling for less than I want" look in a woman's eyes, I will gently challenge her decision and discuss other options. More often than not, she will generally stop and reassess her intended purchase. Together we'll seek out a different piece that not only looks beautiful but also fits! The outcome is always a satisfied customer.

You may be asking, "Why should it matter to you what she buys or how she spends her money?" It's quite simple—I care! I don't want her to settle for looking "all right" when she could look great. It's a matter of conviction in my work, which is more than just a job to me.

When it comes to fit, too small or too big never leaves room for "just right," as Goldilocks learned through trial and error.

"Too small" likes attention. Unfortunately, it's often negative and leads to degrading character labeling and mockery. The "too small" *woman easily ignores such comments because, in her opinion, she looks great!*

On the other hand, the women who prefer the "too big" sizing generally aren't subjected to the same verbal abuse or stares of their "too small" counterparts. This woman runs from the possibility of attracting attention, and her "super-sized" reasoning is something she attempts to justify in one way or another.

The two extremes are both in need of coaching to arrive at the appropriately centered, "just right" fit.

One fall evening, I would put on my coaching cap and assist a young woman whose family was struggling to understand her "too big" sizing mentality.

I noticed a young woman shopping with two children and an older woman. She appeared to be in her late twenties and displayed no regard for her outer physical appearance. Her hair was cut just below her shoulders in no particular style, and she wore no makeup or jewelry. She was wearing what appeared to be a man's oversize sweatshirt and sweatpants, yet I could tell that, underneath the bulky clothes, she had a small frame. Her features were soft and delicate, and she had beautiful blue eyes with lovely, long lashes. The older woman accompanying her was well dressed, and her hair was attractively styled to suit her age. The gentle, warm hues of her blush and lipstick perfectly highlighted her face.

I welcomed them and asked how I could be of help. The young woman pointed to her oversize sweatshirt and, stepping to the right of the stroller, pulled on the sides of her equally large sweatpants and asked, "Do you have any of these?"

The older woman, her mother, Doris, rolled her eyes and said, "Can you help Susan find a variety of clothing she can wear not only at home but also for shopping and functions at the children's school?"

"Why of course I can," I confidently responded.

Susan, clearly annoyed at her mother's request, said, "Mom, there is nothing wrong with these sweats. I don't want to spend a lot of money on fancy clothes. For goodness' sake, I'm home all day."

Doris chimed in, "I am going to pay for everything. I'm tired of seeing you dress like this. There is no reason for it, Susan! Anyway, you are going to want to make friends with other mothers from the school. These sweats will make them wonder why you don't change clothes. Please, Susan, think of putting your best foot forward." Doris directed me once again to help Susan find some new outfits and explained that they had just moved to the area. She wanted Susan to fit in with the other young moms.

I winked at Doris and turned toward Susan. "What do you say? It doesn't get any better than a free shopping spree!"

Susan spoke firmly. "Mom, you don't need to pay for my things. Rick makes good money. I don't feel it's right for me to be wearing all these nice clothes when all I do is take the kids to school, grocery shop, and clean house. I just don't need them! All I really want is two pairs of sweats, and then we can go home!"

Susan turned to me and tried to explain her reasoning. "Pat, I have everything a girl could want. I just don't like to dress up. I want to be comfortable and relaxed. Anyway, no one sees me except the kids and my husband."

"And your father and I and the rest of your family," Doris added, to make her voice heard.

Susan tried to present her side of the situation. "My sisters are professionals, so they have to dress for work. I'm a stay-at-home mom, and I help my husband with the office duties of his business. No one sees me. So why can't I wear what I want? I just don't get what all the fuss is about!"

I hesitated for a moment, trying to find words that would present a balanced perspective, but Susan continued, "My mom even thought I might be anorexic and trying to hide my body, but that's not the issue. I just don't think it's fair for my husband to work so hard and me to be out wasting money on clothes, manicures, haircuts, and everything else women in my neighborhood splurge on."

Doris interjected, "There is *nothing* wrong with having a decent haircut, a manicure, and a cute outfit, Susan! All the young moms in the neighborhood look nice, and I'm sure they will want to get to know you. They're your new neighbors!"

Susan didn't appreciate Doris's comments and gave her a cold stare.

I had clearly become involved in a delicate situation. Both women were adamant in their stances. Since they had openly discussed the issue, I asked some questions.

"Susan, do you know what size you are?"

"Um, I'm about a size four or six."

"Would your husband mind if you came home with some new clothes tonight?"

Susan and Doris looked at one another and laughed. They exclaimed at the same time, "No!" Their response put a spotlight on the situation. It was clear that this was all about Susan and her conviction that this was the way she was supposed to look because she was a stay-at-home mom.

"Ladies, I hear you both loud and clear. So if it's okay with you, I'm going to ask you to have a seat in my reception area, and I am going to put together some classic, casual looks that I think will make you both happy. Will you trust me on this?"

They were both great sports and agreed.

I collected three pairs of denim pants—boot cut, skinny, and boyfriend. I pulled a casual black pant and two cardigans in blue and black. I gathered an assortment of crew and V-neck T-shirts in vibrant colors. I added three long-sleeved cotton shirts with minimal yet attractive prints, two knit pullover sweaters, and three no-iron dress shirts in white, light blue, and black. I selected three cashmere sweaters in attractive styles and a vest instead of a bulky jacket, for our mild fall weather.

I resisted for a moment but decided to include a designer velour sweat suit, which would beautifully replace the sweats Susan was so accustomed to wearing. I went to the handbag department and selected two belts, one in plain, black leather and the other brown with cutout designs. I found a black cross-body bag, which she could wear across her torso or, with little effort, at her side. The bag was big enough to make a fashion statement but small enough to maintain a conservative look. Last, I grabbed three scarves in various textures and designs, which she could use creatively in her hair, around her neck, or as a tie around her purse.

With all these things in hand, I returned to find mother and daughter engaged in conversation. When they saw me, they jumped up from the reception couch and attempted to relieve my arms of all the items. "No girls, really, I'm taking this all inside the fitting room. Susan, come with me!"

Susan didn't hesitate and eagerly followed me. I arranged all the pieces and displayed a variety of looks she could achieve with everything

I had selected for her. Susan seemed excited and couldn't believe I had found everything in such a short time.

"I had to move fast," I teased. "I didn't want you to run off in those sweats without seeing how lovely you could really look!"

My comment struck a chord, and Susan began to share her thoughts about her appearance. "I know I disappoint my mom by how I look. I don't mean to hurt her feelings. I'm just trying to be frugal with our money."

I looked intently at her, eye to eye. "Susan, with all due respect, what you're doing isn't right. You're the beat of your husband's heart. You have a lovely figure. What's wrong with letting him see you looking attractive? Do you ever stop to think how it makes *him* feel to see you dressing in oversized sweats like these all the time? If he works as hard as you say he does, then give him something beautiful to come home to. I'm not saying you have to be all decked out, but for goodness' sake, these gray sweats are not only way too big, but, bottom line, they're grim.

"Sweetheart, you are a role model to your children, and they're watching you! Listen, if this is really about saving money, you need to talk to Rick about ways you can cut back in other areas, but it shouldn't be on you. You've severely underestimated your worth! Taking care of yourself, inside and out, is your responsibility and a gift you give yourself and your family. Your mom has lovingly offered to buy you clothes tonight. Why don't you try these on and see how you look and feel in them?"

Susan looked down for a long moment and then back at me. There were tears in her eyes. "Everything you just said makes sense to me. I never thought of wearing sweats all the time as showing my family that I didn't care about them or myself. I didn't stop to think about how they might feel. I really thought that, by not spending money on myself, I was doing something admirable. I just didn't check in with their thoughts on the matter, and after listening to what you've said, I know I've made a mistake." She began to cry softly, and I stepped out to get her some tissues.

When I returned to the fitting room, I shared my own personal experience. "Susan, when I was a young girl, my mom never cared about her appearance because she said it didn't matter. Sometimes I was downright embarrassed at how she would choose to look. Even as a child, I understood that it was a choice. I grew up knowing I wanted to strive to set a better example than the one I had been shown."

I had bared my heart to Susan, and as she listened, tears continued to stream down her face. "Thank you, Pat. You have really opened my eyes tonight. I want to try on all these clothes." She dried her tears and I said I would check on her in a few minutes.

I walked out to the reception area, and Doris anxiously looked at me. "Oh, Pat, I hope she likes at least one thing you picked out for her. I just don't understand what's happened to my Susan. She has a college degree, and Rick is a wonderful husband, but this is bothering him too. Sweats, sweats, sweats—that's all she'll wear." Doris's lips quivered.

"Doris, I have a feeling Susan is going to like the pieces I selected because they're basics—nothing overdone. But combined they have a great, classic look. It's a good place for her to start."

I touched base with my coworker and then returned to check in on Susan.

"How's it going, Susan?"

She flung the door open and emerged with a huge smile on her face. The boot-cut denim and crew neck T-shirt were her first choices. I grabbed a belt and had her slip it on. Taking the cardigan, I rolled the sleeves so they tied in the front and the base draped against her back. We added the purse, and she had a casual, comfortable, easy-to-wear outfit that looked classic and stylish.

"How does it feel?" I asked.

Susan admired herself in the mirror and said, "Great! I love it! It's easy and comfortable. I want to show my mom."

I couldn't believe the transformation, but it was Susan's family who got the biggest surprise of all.

"Hey, Mom! What do you think?"

Doris looked up, and it was as if she were seeing someone she hadn't seen in years. "Ohhh, Susan," she said, "you look so beautiful!" Doris began to weep.

Susan's mouth fell open. She was clearly impacted by her mother's tears and realized how deeply her choices had affected her.

Susan's little girl said, "Mommy, Mommy, you look so pretty." She reached up to be held and gave Susan a kiss when she picked her up.

Her son came and stood by her. He gently rubbed Susan's arm and smiled proudly at her.

My eyes met with Susan's. We exchanged no words, as the actions of her loved ones said it all.

Susan eagerly went back into the fitting room to try on more clothes. Doris was sincerely appreciative of my efforts and thanked me profusely as she tenderly held my hand. I gave her a hug and said Susan would be coming out in more outfits. She was thrilled!

When I checked in with Susan, her appreciation was more articulate. "I can't remember when someone has spoken to me in a manner as direct as you have tonight. Your words changed me, not just in terms of my clothes, but inside."

I thanked her but gave the credit where it was due. "Susan, this is all your choice. I'm really proud of you. You've made your mom and kids really happy tonight."

Susan smiled and responded that she was proud of herself too. Those were powerful and life-altering words!

Doris enthusiastically purchased everything Susan tried on that night. I asked Susan if she wanted to wear any of it home. She declined, saying she wanted to get the kids to bed and then freshen up to surprise Rick. I gave her my wink of approval. Susan graciously thanked me once again and promised to come back soon.

Doris stood facing me, and taking hold of my hands, she said, "You are something else."

I smiled and told her it was a united effort. It truly had been a wonderful experience for all of us, and we said our good-byes.

The story doesn't end there.

Weeks later, I was in the mall, returning to work, when I saw Susan and her husband, Rick. Susan grabbed Rick's arm and excitedly pointed to me. I could tell she was speaking to him about me. I approached them, and Susan greeted me warmly. She looked like a different woman! She had a nice haircut and manicured nails. Rick graciously put his hand out to shake mine. I introduced myself, and he shared what Susan's shopping visit had meant to both of them.

"Pat, your influence transformed my wife. She came home and apologized for letting herself go. I have to be honest with you, it was starting to become a problem for me. I don't know what would have happened to our marriage down the road if you hadn't helped her that night."

"Rick, believe it or not, this behavior is quite common. But once Susan realized what was going on, she decided to take action and overcome that mind-set. I'm really happy for all of you!"

Susan reached over and hugged me. Rick said I had permission to sell Susan anything I thought would look great on her. "It's carte blanche when she shops with you."

I laughed and told him I was flattered by his confidence, and I would always do my best for her.

Susan and Doris came back to shop for the holidays, and in the spring, we put together a beautiful wardrobe for her. She confessed she had thrown out the oversize sweats and, in hindsight, couldn't believe she had allowed herself to settle into such a dreadful look.

I shared that it wasn't so much that sweats were a bad thing in themselves. It was the need to wear them like a uniform and to substitute them for daily wear that created a problem. The same can be said for women who wear active wear all day, every day. She understood, but for the sake of never retreating back into a nasty habit, she'd thrown them away. Her actions caused her to radiate a newfound self-esteem. It was obvious she was on track and felt comfortable being who she was at this stage in her life!

Susan's story ended "just right," but there are other women who likewise continue to struggle in this area. Remember, it's not about looking "all right." Anyone can do that, because it doesn't require much. Instead, choose to stretch! Make a conscientious decision to reevaluate where you may need to make changes in your wardrobe. It doesn't have to cost a lot of money, and if need be, ask for help from a professional.

The outcome will validate your efforts.

The Child Stylist: My Job Is Challenged

It never ceases to amaze me when women bring children shopping and ask their advice on fit and clothing selections. It's disturbing to hear a woman plead with the child to accept a piece of clothing she likes and then give in to the child's contrary opinion. More often than not, the woman has issues she wants to address with clothing, which can create an unhealthy mind-set for a child. Furthermore, a child has no understanding of a woman's fully developed body or of the dynamics of dressing to please her partner. Engaging youngsters as personal stylists is not a good idea, and this story provides a glimpse into some of the reasons why.

I was in the fitting room area organizing racks when a woman called out to me and said, "Excuse me, what do you think of this shirt? My daughter really likes it on me, but I'm not sure."

I introduced myself, and before I could comment on the shirt, the daughter, who was approximately eight years old, said, "I picked it out, and I like it." She gave me a smug look and crossed her arms, daring me to defy her selection.

"I'm sorry," I said to the mother, "what was your name?"

"Oh, I'm Olivia, and this is my daughter, Calla."

I nodded my head in acknowledgment and answered her question.

"Olivia, that shirt is much too big on you, and I think we can do better with another color."

Calla responded by telling me that big shirts were in style and that she liked it. I was determined not to have a clothing discussion with the little girl and directed my body language and words entirely toward her mom.

"Olivia, I have another shirt in mind, which I think will be much more flattering. This shirt is simply too big. You have excess fabric draping all over. It's supposed to fit like this," I said as I showed her where the piece was failing her.

"Oh, that's really good advice," Olivia responded. "I see exactly what you're saying. Would you mind looking at some of the other things Calla and I have picked out? My husband and I are going to Florida in two weeks, and I'm trying to find some cute outfits to wear."

"No! I don't want her to look at them," Calla blurted out and gave me a dirty look, which her mom didn't see.

After the clothing review, I removed all but two pieces. "I'm going to bring you a number of selections you can mix and match, as well as some denim I think you will really enjoy."

Olivia was very excited. Calla, however, was not and told her mom I acted like a know-it-all. Olivia said nothing, and I promised to return within a few minutes.

Keeping in mind that her upcoming trip was a romantic getaway with her husband, I selected a few sexy pieces I thought would be flattering. When I returned, I knocked, and Calla opened the door slightly and peeped at me with one eye.

"Honey, my hands are full. I need you to open the door all the way."

She and her mom had a brief tug of war with the door, and at last, I entered and presented the clothing to Olivia, explaining how each piece could work for her.

Calla decided to create a distraction with the mirrored panels. *Slam* ... shut! ... *Slam* ... open! Olivia was either choosing to ignore her daughter or didn't care that she was going to break the mirrors.

Gently touching Olivia's arm, I turned to Calla and politely, yet firmly said, "Please, honey, stop! You are going to break the mirrors, and the shattered glass could hurt us."

Calla stopped but made another face at me.

Olivia, however, said nothing, as she was too busy slipping on one of the tops I had just brought her.

"Oh, I love this! I'm definitely getting this," she said excitedly.

I excused myself to finish tending to another customer, who was ready and waiting for me at my counter. Olivia asked me to hurry back to provide her with my opinion.

Minutes later, I knocked on the door, and Calla told me to go away!

"Oh Calla, she's just trying to help me. Now you just stop." Olivia opened the door, beaming with joy. "Look at these pants," she cried gleefully. They make my butt look great! I'm getting these too."

I asked if she had tried on the blue, embroidered sundress.

She shuffled through the pieces, found it, and put it on.

"Isn't it beautiful? It's one of my favorites because it's such a romantic piece. Your husband is going to love it," I said.

She loved it too, until Calla remarked that it made her look fat and that her daddy wouldn't like it. Olivia immediately turned and looked at me in a panic!

I was taken aback at how Calla had been able to arouse such a reaction from her mother. I reassuringly placed my hand on Olivia's shoulder and said that, as adults, we knew better. Why, she could wear that dress to scrub the tub, and her husband would just love it. We both understood and started to laugh. Calla was clearly out of the loop and didn't appreciate it.

Olivia said she was thrilled we had met. "Finally I have found someone who is teaching me how to dress!"

These were words I appreciated, but Calla did not. She dropped to the floor and began to cry.

"I don't like her! She's ruined our shopping trip!"

I thought it best to leave the two alone and said, "Olivia, take your time in making your final selections. I will be at my counter if you need anything."

As I walked away, I overheard Olivia telling Calla that she loved the way the clothes made her look and feel, and she was going to buy them all. Calla, still crying and whining, repeated that her daddy wasn't going to like them because she hadn't picked them out. Olivia briefly found her "Mom Hat" and responded firmly and confidently, "Daddy is going to love me in these clothes!"

"Well, I don't. They're ugly. The ones I picked were better," Calla bitterly snapped back.

"Well, maybe you can help me find some shoes," Olivia conceded, in an attempt to pacify her.

Out on the sales floor, a woman approached me. She had been in another fitting room and had overheard my conversations with Olivia and Calla. "That child needs a good spanking or, better yet, to be left at home."

Another woman who also had been eavesdropping in the fitting rooms said she agreed. The two women vented their opinions to one another and proceeded to shop as newfound friends.

Olivia eventually emerged from the fitting room and announced she was going to purchase all but three of the pieces she had tried on. She was delighted and expressed her appreciation.

"Pat, I want to thank you so much for your help tonight. I feel like I'm buying grown-up clothes. I'm so happy with everything! But unfortunately, Calla isn't. She's mad at me for not buying what she picked out and said you and I were mean to her."

Calla stood sulking behind her mom. She had clearly been rude, disrespectful, and annoying, but the parent within me rose up and I decided to have a chat with her.

"Honey, I know you like to shop with Mommy, but there's something very important you need to know. It really matters to me how your mommy looks, and that's why I had to tell her the truth about some of the clothes you had picked out for her. I want her to look beautiful, and I know you want that too! The clothes your mommy is buying make her feel happy and special. Isn't that what you want for her too?"

Calla nodded in agreement and gave me a hug. Olivia smiled, as did the ladies who'd commented on the situation earlier, who were within earshot of the conversation.

I escorted Olivia to the counter and rang up a generous sale, but equally important, I earned the respect of both mother and daughter.

A future shopping visit with Olivia and Calla proved to be quite delightful. Olivia commented that her husband had loved her vacation wardrobe, especially the sexy sundress.

"Now I need your help picking a cute outfit for a concert we're going to this weekend," she said.

"Great! I have some new pieces that would be perfect," I responded.

Olivia asked Calla if she wanted to help us.

"No, Mommy. That's Pat's job. I just want to sit here and color."

Calla's response took Olivia and me completely by surprise. We turned to one another and couldn't help but smile.

A valuable style lesson had been learned!

The Pesky Itch:
Meeting the Needs of My Customer

Customer service requires numerous capabilities. My clients know I will do anything to make their shopping experience a great one. Did I say anything? I did, didn't I! My client, Maggie, can attest to that!

Maggie was shopping for sweaters to keep her warm and looking great on her upcoming fishing trip with her family. In her sixties, Maggie is active and lives life to the fullest. When her favorite designer's product goes on sale, I'm sure to see her in the store.

"Hi, Pat," I heard her call out as she went into the fitting room. "I'll be out in a few minutes," she added.

"Not to worry, dear. I'll be right here. Enjoy!"

Some twenty minutes later, she emerged with her selections. Smiling broadly, she appeared to have come and conquered! In her arms were numerous pieces in one of her favorite colors, cobalt blue. It looks stunning on her and compliments her bright blue eyes. I promised to be with her in a few minutes, as the line was long. She kindly assured me that she didn't mind, and we would chat when it was her turn.

And soon it was. Maggie was at my counter and, as always, I gave her a welcoming hug and greeting. "How are you? What's new and exciting?"

Maggie's response didn't disappoint. As she proceeded to tell me about her new little puppy and upcoming trip, I took to the task of removing the security sensors, tagging each piece, and wrapping her items.

Suddenly, Maggie began to shift her stance and said, "Ooh, ooooh, I've got an itch." She quickly came around to my side of the counter and stood with her back toward me. "Quick! I've got an itch. Scratch my back! It's right in the middle." She wiggled and twisted as if doing so would somewhat lessen the nuisance of the itch. She had moved so quickly that I was taken off guard by her urgency.

"Hurry, scratch!" she said.

I dropped the scanner on the counter and did as I was told. "Up, up! To the right! No, down just a little toward the center. Up, up! Just a little more. Next to the shoulder blade."

I was trying my best to track the evasive itch as she verbally directed me toward it, when at last I heard, "*That's it*! Ahh, yes, right there! *Scratch*! Oh, that feels great! Ahh, thank you!"

I continued to scratch as she stood with her back to me.

At that moment, a woman coming out of the fitting room noticed the scenario and said, "Wow! Now *that's* customer service!"

I smiled; nodded; and, yes, continued to scratch. I looked over at my line and saw the faces of women observing me scratching Maggie's back. Some were laughing, while others had raised eyebrows and dropped jaws. I smiled and mouthed that I would be with them shortly, and in return, they nodded in understanding.

Maggie couldn't have cared less, as she was being relieved of the pesky itch. After a bit, she felt relief, turned to me with a smiling face, and thanked me. She walked around the counter, resumed her spot, and proclaimed, "What service!"

I laughed and said, "Anything for you, Maggie!"

The ladies standing in line smiled at one another, and one called out, "Do you do manicures?"

"Only on myself. Sorry." I responded with a wink.

I quickly finished the transaction and Maggie was set to go. "Have a great trip, dear. I want to hear all about it."

She smiled and said, "You're the best!"

"So are you, Maggie, so are you!" I responded and waved good-bye.

I called to the next customer in line and she placed her selections on the counter. She looked intently at me and said, "I come to this store a lot and I always see you working with customers. *Now*, I get it! That was unlike anything I have ever seen a salesperson do for a customer. That lady felt so comfortable with you, and you willingly scratched her back. I want to write a customer comment about this."

The woman who was standing behind her in line approached the counter and added, "I agree! At first it was funny, but then I saw the sweetness in it. I mean, look at you. Here you are, all dressed up, and you're scratching a customer's back. I love it!"

I laughed and thanked them for their words of appreciation. Granted, scratching Maggie's back isn't in my job description, but kindness and yielding to the individual needs of a customer really do matter. I never thought scratching her back would be so impactful, but apparently it was, because other women also commented kindly about it.

You might be thinking that scratching someone's back isn't something you would choose to do at work. Well, it may be unusual but that's okay! I'm going to put weight on the saying that, when you scratch someone's back, someone will, at one time or another, scratch yours in return. The truth is, every effort I extend toward my customers will hold its own reward, and that is good enough for me.

Fitting Room Leftovers:
Thrown Away and Never Saved

Customers leave personal belongings in our fitting rooms on a daily basis, and we promptly take them to the lost and found department. However, when items such as dirty diapers, food, tissues, coffee cups, and other types of containers are found, they are disposed of without hesitation. My partners and I are diligent in maintaining the cleanliness of our department for the common good.

Unfortunately, despite our best intentions, there was one shopper who didn't see eye to eye with our cleanly methods and demanded an answer.

Our fitting rooms were experiencing a high volume of traffic, with many women trying on clothes. My partner, Shelley, and I were assisting customers and tending to numerous tasks requiring our attention. I noticed a woman, perhaps in her late twenties, who had been shopping for quite a while. She had refused our assistance and been in and out of the fitting room numerous times. She approached my counter and announced she was ready to check out.

As I processed her transaction, we chatted about the items she had selected. She had been given a gift card, and with a Caribbean vacation approaching in two weeks, she was buying new clothes to take on her trip.

"It's been a long time since I've shopped for myself. I'm going to throw out my old clothes and replace them with all of this," she said, proudly pointing to the beautiful assortment of clothing.

I commended her for taking such positive steps and explained that wardrobe renovation didn't come easily to most women. Emotional deterrents often hold them back from clearing out the old and bringing in the new. She smiled as I assured her that she was on the right track! I completed the transaction of four shopping bags and wished her a wonderful vacation.

Shelley and I continued to work happily as we made headway with a large rack of clothing that had to get back out on the sales floor.

An hour or so had passed when I noticed the same woman I had assisted earlier now back in my department. Standing by the clothing rack near the fitting room entrance, I welcomed her once again. I remarked that I admired her shopping tenacity. She laughed and said she had found other pieces that had caught her eye and wanted to try them on.

Within seconds, however, she reappeared at the fitting room entrance and let out a loud, disgruntled huff. She was clearly agitated; she raised her hands, clenched into fists, and pumped them up and down. Shelley and I had no idea what was wrong and were about to ask, when she looked directly at Shelley and demanded to know what had happened to her organic bottled drink. Shelley and I looked at one another and back at the woman. She raised her voice and repeated, "What did you do with my drink?"

We were stunned at the aggressive tone in her voice, and Shelley, who wouldn't hurt a fly, gently responded, "I'm not sure. We both cleared out the rooms a number of times. I did find an empty bottle of water and a bottled drink, but it was practically empty. I'm sorry if it was yours. I thought it had been intentionally left in the room to be thrown away."

The woman appeared to be not only insulted but also shocked at Shelley's admission. She furiously pumped her clenched fists up and down and yelled, "*What*! No! I did not intentionally leave it there for you to *throw away*. I was going to *drink it*! There was still some left in the bottle. Don't you realize those drinks are *expensive*?"

We were astounded at what she was saying. Shelley had indeed thrown the bottle away but with no ill will intended. "I'm so sorry," she sincerely responded.

The woman continued, "Well, where did you put it? Can you—"

I knew where she was going with that question and immediately interrupted her, "No! It was thrown in the trash, which housekeeping already collected."

The woman's facial expression was one of disbelief. She could not understand how the organic drink, which she had left in the fitting room over an hour ago, could be gone! Thrown in the garbage! Disgusted with our explanation, she angrily replied, "Who do you think you are, throwing away people's belongings? You need to keep things like that in case people want them!"

I wanted to say they didn't make refrigerators that big but restrained my tongue and responded with the truth. "Ma'am, you left your drink in our fitting room over an hour ago. For safety and sanitation reasons we don't save drinks or food items. I'm very sorry, but your drink–it's gone."

I tapped Shelley's arm and turned to the full clothing rack. A rattled Shelley whispered, "I didn't think anyone would want a drink that was left behind like that. Who knows what someone could do to it."

"Sweetie," I said, "we simply do not save food or drinks, ever! You did nothing wrong. Come on. Let's get to work. We have clothes to rack."

Although Shelley was hurt because of the way she'd been spoken to, she knew she had to let it go.

Minutes later the woman came out of the fitting room, still holding a bitter grudge. I expressed our regrets once again and wished her a good evening but received no reply. I went into the fitting room to do a check and found she had left us her calling card. The clothes she had taken in to try on were all turned inside out and scattered all over the floor. I wasn't surprised. Some people can be quite petty when things don't go their way.

These are the challenging moments my partners and I are exposed to throughout our day. The work we love and enjoy sometimes pricks us with a nasty thorn. Shelley and I took comfort in our partnership and the absurdity of the situation. Shelley wondered out loud how much organic drinks must cost. I, on the other hand, wondered what was *in* the organic potion because, whatever it was, that woman obviously needed a double.

Postpartum Predicament: A New Look for Mama

In my opinion, becoming a new mom is one of the most exciting events in a woman's life. There are so many issues that must be anticipated and addressed in nine short months. However, the physical changes due to pregnancy and childbirth can create challenges that a woman can't fully comprehend until after her baby is born. One fall evening, a young couple would confront this reality in my department.

They didn't have a sign that read, "Parents of Newborn," but it was obvious to this mother of three. I was confident of my assumption because this couple, whose eyes declared sleep deprivation, was pushing a pristine stroller with a massive diaper bag. They walked directly to the reception area with their sleeping infant and got situated. I congratulated them and offered my assistance should they need anything. The young dad, who had obviously come to offer moral support, encouraged the young mom to begin her shopping, which she did with hesitation.

She walked about, touching the clothing. However, nothing was captivating enough for her to pull it from the racks. She went through the majority of the department within ten quick minutes and then began to rummage through the clearance racks. She lacked expression and when I made eye contact with her and smiled, she immediately turned away.

Her frustration was becoming more evident as she firmly flicked the hangers. It was as though I could read her thoughts: "Remember when you could wear something like this?" and "Who wears a size four? Not me, that's for sure."

Eventually, she picked out two oversized sweaters in black, of course, as well as a cable-knit sweaterdress, again in black. She proceeded to the reception area and showed her husband what she had selected. He enthusiastically asked her to come out when she had them on. She nodded in response and reluctantly entered the fitting room. Minutes later, she came out in one of the sweaters.

Her husband sat up attentively and said, "Do you like it? It looks nice."

She said nothing. It appeared to be a struggle for her just to come out and show him.

He repeated his question, "Do you like it?"

She shrugged her shoulders, turned, and went back in the fitting room. A short time passed, and she came out in the other bulky sweater. She stood in front of him looking as though she were about to cry. He knew the shopping trip was taking its toll on her.

"Babe, you look fine. You just had a baby. It's a nice sweater. If you like it, I want you to buy it!"

She shook her head in disgusted discouragement with her body and retreated to the fitting room. I looked at her husband, and he sighed as he ran his fingers through his hair in helplessness. The situation was equally difficult for him. He wanted to be supportive, but it wasn't working.

Shortly thereafter, she came out in the cable-knit dress, and it was indeed the final straw. She began to express harsh and cruel thoughts about herself and her size. He tried to stop her, but her words overpowered his. She was a force within herself, like a hurricane. Her words stripped bare any self-esteem she had once had and left him in a state of withdrawal, desperately wanting to seek shelter. She felt angry and betrayed by her very self, and her tears began to flow.

It was time for me to intervene!

"Hi, my name is Pat, and I'm a mom. I know exactly how you feel right now, and I promise you, this is not a forever situation. I've held back and watched you select items you thought would work for you. But the truth is, big, black, and bulky is not the solution to your figure right now.

Will you give me the opportunity to select a few pieces and show you just how lovely you can look? Just give me five minutes."

She let out one of the deepest sighs I have ever heard, and her husband looked at me with eyes pleading for help. I asked her approximate size and invited her to have a seat.

"Five minutes," I repeated with a wink.

I quickly collected different pieces, which would complement her skin tone and flatter her shape. I returned with four complete outfits, and as I showed them to her, she began to relax, and I could see hope in her eyes!

"Would you like to take these into the fitting room and try them on?" I asked.

She looked at her husband for reassurance.

"Go on, babe. Get anything you want. I love you."

She stood and followed me back to the room, where she turned to me and said, "Thank you for being so understanding. I didn't want to ask for help because I was embarrassed."

I smiled and, putting my hand on her shoulder, said, "Honey, wanting to look good should never cause you to feel embarrassed. Let's have you try these on, and then come out and model them for us."

It took a few minutes, but she finally came out. She seemed almost shy at first, but her husband extended his hand toward her and said, "Wow, that's my girl. You look great, babe!"

"Do you really like it?" she asked.

"Absolutely! You look beautiful. I love it," he tenderly responded.

They smiled lovingly at one another, and the tension that had permeated the lounge area disappeared. I felt it was important to explain why the outfit was working for her and how to pull the same look with other pieces she might have at home. She nodded in understanding and expressed appreciation for the coaching moment.

She continued to stand admiring the outfit when I said, "Hey, Mama, let's see some more good-looking outfits on you."

They both laughed, and she excitedly went back in to try on another selection.

The scenario repeated itself at least three more times as she was mixing and matching the different pieces. Each time she exuded more and more confidence. I left them to discuss their purchasing options, after which she quickly went to change her clothes.

Her husband called me over and said, "Pat, I want to thank you for your help tonight. I was so worried when she lost control and started crying. I didn't know what I was going to do."

"It's a time of transition. Your love and support is going to get her through. Trust me, you're all going to be just fine," I assured him.

She had selected a delicate, soft pink, ruffled sweater with a white sparkle camisole; a light blue, chiffon top; a black, V-neck shirt she could accessorize with a scarf, as I had shown her; and a pair of boot-cut denim.

When they approached my counter, she was like a different woman! The woman who had come into my department, the one who was hesitant, insecure, and intimidated to shop, was not the one standing before me. This was a happy young woman, excited and eager to wear her new clothes and proud to be a new mom.

The mood was joyous as I completed the transaction and walked around the counter to hand her the shopping bag.

"Thank you so much," she said. "I can't begin to express how renewed I feel. I'm so glad you were here to help me."

I reached out, gave her a quick hug, and noticed that their baby girl was starting to stir in her stroller.

"You are so welcome," I said. "But before you go, I have a big favor to ask of you. Promise me that, when you wear these clothes, you will do it with lots of sass." I gave her a wink, and we all laughed.

She confidently looked me in the eye and said, "I promise you, I will!"

And you know what, I believed her!

The Secret:
Out in the Open

Sometimes we hold a personal secret and dread the thought of it ever being exposed. The countless possible repercussions create fear, anxiety, and shame.

One evening, a woman shopping in my department would come face-to-face with her secret. Would she choose to break the binding chains it had created in her life? Or would she walk away with its grip firmly holding her and her family in silent bondage?

It was Friday evening and I had already spent half an hour with my customer. We had become acquainted on a previous visit and reunited to find her an outfit for a family gathering taking place the next day. Barbara came from a large family, and looking her best was always an obligation at such events. To fall short in that regard would be disrespectful, and she wasn't about to go there. While she and I searched for some options, her daughter, Christina, went to the juniors' department to browse through the denim.

"Make sure you don't stay long. I'm going to need you here in just about twenty minutes," Barbara said to her.

"I know, Mom, I know," Christina responded as she walked away.

Barbara and I enjoyed chatting and getting to know one another as we selected numerous pieces for her to try on. We went to the fitting room where I arranged everything and encouraged her to enjoy the process. She said she would try but, due to some recent weight gain, it wasn't going to be as pleasurable as she would like.

I cupped my ears and shook my head, saying, "I don't want to hear any of that. You look just fine, and this is for the here and now. Just think of the party and all the fun you're going to have."

She laughed and promised she would do her best as she closed the door.

Barbara appeared to be in her early forties. She was a very striking woman whose mannerisms reflected style and elegance, yet she was very sweet and genuine.

Within minutes she came out in a dramatic black-and-red dress. She was in full command of it. Just beautiful!

I'm in love with this dress," she exclaimed. "I'm not even going to bother with the other outfits."

"Barbara, it's just stunning, but do try the other pieces on. You may be surprised and find one you like equally as well."

"Oh, but I *love* this dress," she said, as she hugged herself in it.

I laughed but stood by my suggestion because of the different looks the other pieces could offer.

Sure enough, she selected two more outfits in addition to the dress. She was on cloud nine. I collected her clothing, and as we walked toward the counter, she began to get anxious as to where Christina could be.

"Don't worry. I'll call the juniors' department and have them track her down."

"Could you, Pat? I want to pay for everything all at once. In the meantime, I will try to call her, and let's see who reaches her first."

Her comment reminded me that, even in this day of multiple methods of communication, it can still be so difficult to get in touch with someone.

I called the department, described Christina and asked if someone there could relay the message that her mom was ready to go. The associate who answered said she would advise her counter partner, who was currently with Christina. Barbara also reached Christina, who said she would head back shortly, as she was just finishing trying on some jeans.

I asked Barbara if she wanted to look for some accessories. She hesitated and then firmly decided no; she wanted me to start processing everything so she could get going.

"I still have to wrap the present, touch up my nails, and tweeze my eyebrows. You know how it is before a family gathering. It all has to be perfect!"

I understood and began the process of wrapping and hanging her purchases. I made small talk about the party, but Barbara was clearly distracted and called Christina once more.

"Where is that girl? She said she would be here a few minutes ago."

I also called again and was told Christina had left. It was only the next department over, so she should have been here by now. Barbara wasn't getting a response on Christina's phone, which created a heightened sense of urgency. She kept turning her head in search of Christina, and I found myself getting caught up in her emotion.

"I am really getting angry at her. Where is she? I don't have time for this nonsense."

"Barbara, I'm sorry. I would have her paged, but it's only permitted for an actual emergency."

A line was forming, and my partner was anticipating my assistance. I had delayed as much as I could. My preparations were done, and I had rung her items. Barbara was now frantic, "Where *is* she?"

"Would you prefer I suspend the transaction and you can search for her?" I asked.

"No. I'm just wondering where she is. She *knows* I need her here right now."

I wasn't sure what more I could do. Once again, I offered to suspend the transaction, but she shook her head in refusal. "Well, then, your things are set to go. The amount is $264.24."

She panicked and turned, looking in every direction for Christina. There was an unsettling moment when she just stood staring at me. She quickly began to search and fumble through her purse, as though she had lost something.

"Barbara, is everything all right?" I gently asked.

She neither looked at me nor responded to my question. She just continued shuffling through her purse. I didn't know exactly what she was looking for, so I suggested methods of payment.

"It's okay if you don't have your card. I can look it up."

"No, I can't use my cards. I only have a check," she said, quite flustered.

"Oh, well, that's fine. There's no problem with a check."

"I'm trying to find my checkbook," she said, keeping her head down and looking into her handbag. It was taking minutes, rather than seconds, to find it. She dialed for Christina again, with no success. Her hands were shaking, and I noticed beads of perspiration on her face as she finally pulled out her checkbook.

I tried to act nonchalant, but there was obviously something wrong. I offered her a pen.

"No, I have my own!" she said. She continued to alternate between looking every which way for her daughter and rummaging through her handbag.

My partner coughed loudly in an attempt to get an explanation as to what was causing the delay. I looked at her and turned to look at the line. It was five deep. Barbara looked up right at that moment and saw I was holding the line for her.

"Here! Here's my pen," she said.

She opened her checkbook and then just stood there with her head down, frozen for what again seemed to be minutes.

"Barbara, is there something wrong? Can I help you?"

She slowly lifted her head, and I saw tears in her eyes. She was breathing deeply and trembling.

"Barbara, honey, what is it?"

"Pat, I'm so sorry to have made you wait, and look, all those people are waiting too. I'm so sorry. I'm so embarrassed to tell you this. You're probably going to think I'm a stupid idiot loser, but I don't know how to write a check. I don't know how to read or write." And with that she let out a stream of tears. She hung her head in shame and wept.

I stood motionless for a moment and then walked around the counter. "Barbara, it's okay. I thought there was something *wrong* with you."

Through her tears, she chuckled at my statement, because, in her heart and mind, she felt there *was* something wrong with her.

"Barbara, this is fixable in the short and long term. I will help you. I will show you how to write a check. Don't worry! Do you know how to write letters and numbers?"

"Yes, I know how to write them but not very well. I don't know how to write words, especially the words for numbers."

She let out a deep sigh as I stood close to her and repeated, "This is fixable. Together you and I are going to write this check. You are going to do something you have always been afraid to do."

I asked her to open her checkbook to a blank check. I explained every detail on it and had her repeat what I said. I showed her how we would write the date with just numbers. I was very thorough and explained that each month could be identified numerically. Since the month of September was the ninth month of the year, it would be identified by the number 9. The number of the day was 24 and the number for the year was 2010. I wrote it out for her on a piece of cash register tape, 9/24/2010, and I also showed her how it appeared in writing, September 24, 2010.

"Now, you write it numerically on the check," I said.

She took a deep breath, looked anxiously at me, and wrote the numbers carefully and slowly in the allotted space. She exhaled and looked at me for assurance when she completed that task.

"Excellent! You did it perfectly!" I said.

We proceeded with the other details of the check until it was completely filled out.

My partner by now realized I was dealing with a delicate situation, and she had marvelously taken care of the line in a quick, orderly manner. We looked at one another with merciful understanding.

Barbara's tears and trembling body were gradually calming. She was softly smiling and realizing what she had actually accomplished. The exposure of her secret had left her emotionally and physically spent. I explained how the checks were processed and that I would be returning hers to her so she could take it home for review. Barbara looked completely exhausted, as though she had just finished a final exam in school. I went around to my side of the register and finished the transaction, and together we stepped away from the counter.

"Barbara, do you want to know something that you and I have in common?"

"What?" she asked wearily.

"The very first check I ever wrote in my life was to this store! I was eighteen years old and had purchased two pairs of jeans. And you know what else? When I was in high school, I tutored children at the local grammar school who couldn't read and struggled to write because of it. I was supposed to help you today, Barbara, because today was the day you were meant to be set free from this secret."

She started to cry and held my hands tightly. "I know I need to learn, but my shame stops me. I don't know where to go and ask for help without feeling like a fool. I don't even know if I can learn anymore."

"Of course you can learn! I just showed you how to write a check, and you did it. You are fully capable. You need to practice writing your numbers and letters and become confident doing that. Just practice over and over. There are adult education sites that will guide you to the right place for help, depending on where you live. You don't need to be afraid, because they only work with adults. They want to help you and will gladly do so!" I assured her that, by taking that first step, with time and effort, she would enjoy learning to read and write.

She hugged me deeply in appreciation. We both let out a big sigh and then broke out in laughter, which further calmed our emotions.

Although she was physically spent, she proceeded to explain that, every time she shopped, Christina had to come with her. She would make an excuse, and Christina would write the check for her. She had tried using credit cards but was afraid because she couldn't keep track of the codes and pin numbers.

"Once, when they asked me for the security code, I couldn't read it and panicked. I left everything on the counter and walked out. This is why I need Christina with me when I shop."

"Barbara, it doesn't have to be that way anymore! Promise me that you will call one of the schools. Don't be afraid. Just think, it's going to open a whole new world for you!"

She nodded her head in agreement, and just then, she saw Christina walking in the adjacent portion of the women's department.

"Christina! Christina!" She excitedly motioned for her to come over.

Christina was flustered. "Mom, where have you been? I went to the counter near the fitting rooms where you were trying on clothes and couldn't find you. I don't know why, but I couldn't get reception on my phone, so I couldn't call you."

We looked at her in relief. Everyone was where they were supposed to be, and now the story could be told.

"Look, Christina," Barbara cried, her eyes gleaming with unbounded pride. "I wrote a check! Pat taught me how to write a check." She held the check out for Christina to appreciate. "She showed me where everything goes, and look, I wrote it!"

Christina, who was at most sixteen, was shocked that I had learned her mother's secret.

"I'm so sorry, Mom. I went looking for you and I couldn't find you. But really, you wrote a check? Wow! Let me see it!"

Christina examined her mother's work, and they hugged one another.

I explained to Christina about the resources available for her mom and that she would need to encourage her to pursue them. "Honey, if you help your mom take these initial steps, you are going to release yourself and other members of your family from carrying this burden as well."

They both agreed and promised to take action. Barbara and Christina chatted with me for a bit longer and then prepared to leave.

"Pat, I will never be able to thank you for what you did for me tonight. Christina and I will get to work on this so we don't have to live like this anymore."

They hugged me and I wished them a great time at the party.

My shift was over shortly after Barbara and Christina left the store. As I drove home, I realized I was still slightly shaken by the incident. It had served to remind me once again to never assume that an individual's appearance reflects his or her innermost needs.

I thought about how the timing of the situation and my previous experience had made me a perfect match for Barbara. I thought back to the children I had tutored in high school, as well as my own, whom I had taught to read and write. Even though it had been years since I had tutored someone, helping Barbara reminded me how wonderful it made me feel inside.

Barbara would seek me out on future visits and share her progress. Her biggest hurdles of fear and shame were behind her, and she slowly blossomed with each step she took going forward.

Fads:
They're More Than Just Clothes

My daughter, Amy, and I were talking one night about a video featuring the fad "coning." Amy laughed as she described the scene.

A server at a fast-food restaurant hands an ice cream cone to a young man. The base of the cone has been carefully wrapped with a protective cover, and the server also provides two napkins in case of dripping. Little does she know, her thoughtfulness is going to be entirely disregarded.

The young man, a college student in his early twenties, proceeds to grab the ice cream rather than the crispy cone, thus "coning." The ice cream squishes through his fingers and onto the counter. At first the server isn't quite sure how to respond as she stares at him and the counter, now generously covered in ice cream and chunks of the shattered cone.

In the background, you hear the outrageous laughter of his friends who have come along to witness the fad in action. The prankster, who has remained straight-faced throughout, proceeds to lick and smack his fingers and even swipes the counter to get another taste of the melting vanilla treat as he turns to leave.

The server, who by now has caught on to the prank, is quite annoyed and clearly disgusted as she is last seen wiping the mess off her counter and coping with disgruntled customers delayed in her food line.

My colleague, Danielle, and I were once subjected to something like this.

It was Memorial Day weekend, and the store was busy with customers shopping for clothes for the warm weather ahead.

Our counter is tucked well behind a high-traffic area, so we were taken off guard when a large group of people surrounded it and began to talk all at once.

Finally, the voice of one of the men in the group dominated the others. "There's a woman lying lifeless on the ground under one of the displays over there. You need to do something."

My counter partner and I worked instinctively and took on the task. Danielle calmed the group and told me she would call the office and security, while I quickly went to locate the woman.

I have to be honest with you, I said a prayer and began putting all my first aid cue cards in mental order. No one in the group accompanied me, since they had children with them and were assuming the worst.

As I approached the area, I saw the young woman on the ground. It was a very odd scene because people were literally stepping over her and doing absolutely nothing to assist her.

When I was approximately five feet away, I went into observation mode. I examined the area to see if anything had fallen near her. I looked for cuts or blood. She had no possessions with her. She appeared to be alone. Her coloring looked normal. I was putting pieces together from a purely visual standpoint.

I was about a foot away when the most crucial information I needed in order to address the situation came to mind. I had recently read an article that would help me resolve this "emergency" quite effectively.

I kneeled down next to the blonde-haired girl. She, like the young man in the coning incident, appeared to be in her early twenties. She was lying perfectly straight with her arms tightly at her sides. I leaned in close to her and spoke firmly. "Young lady, this is no place for you to plank! I know you may think it's funny, but it's not! You need to get up right this second!"

I stayed next to her on bended knee, and a huge smile came across her face. She opened her big, blue eyes, which twinkled mischievously at me and said, "It's a school project," assuming that would make it entirely permissible.

I continued in the same firm tone, "That may be so, but you need to do it somewhere else. You have already upset a number of our customers. I want you up, *now*! Security is on the way."

One thing about fad enthusiasts is that they never perform alone, and I could hear the hearty laughter coming from her friends. For a moment, she looked disappointed, as though I had just spoiled the outcome of her final grade, but she quickly stood and raised her arms in victory. Her friends cheered and roared in approval as she approached them, and they retold the event from their perspective.

A manager promptly arrived and led them out of the store.

This had all happened within a few short minutes. I quickly returned to my counter, where everyone was awaiting my report. Danielle could tell by the look on my face it had been a prank. She smiled at me, and I back at her, relieved I hadn't needed to use my first aid skills.

I explained to the concerned group that they had witnessed a fad called "planking." The adults expressed irritation at having been duped, but it was the shaken voice of one child, who innocently said, "I didn't like that joke. It scared me," which presented the situation in an entirely different perspective.

Surprisingly, it was then that the adults began to recount their own teenage and college hijinks and started to laugh. "You have to give her credit for scaring us to death," said the man who had been the speaker for the group.

But the voice of reason spoke up once again from his little girl, "It wasn't funny, Daddy."

Danielle and I gracefully dismissed everyone and took a proud moment to appreciate our method of teamwork.

That night, as I drove home, I thought back to "my days." Would I have done anything like that? I won't tell! But the fact remained; the young woman was going to have a story to share with her grandkids about the night she pranked with her plank. And I have to tell you, I smiled at her in hindsight.

A Matter of Opinion: When Changing One Counts

Unfortunately, there are many misconceptions regarding the tasks my coworkers and I perform in retail. For example, it's said we are just cashiers, and our work is mindless and meaningless. It is assumed we have no goals or ambitions, suffer from low self-esteem, and therefore "deserve" to pick up clothes left on fitting room floors. Furthermore, we are used as visual examples, for warning daughters to straighten up, lest they "turn out" like one of us.

Such assumptions, comments, and behaviors can be hurtful to the heart, shocking to hear, and disturbing to experience. However, those of us who delight in our work gain personal satisfaction in sharing our professional talents. We know there are customers who sincerely appreciate the assistance and knowledge we provide.

One evening as I worked alone in my department, I would face the challenge of redirecting perceptions of me and my work.

As two women lingered over a table of folded sweaters, I welcomed them to my department. I briefly explained our promotions and offered my assistance should they need anything.

Neither one lifted her head to acknowledge me, and one of them said dismissively, "Okay."

It just so happened they were the only shoppers in my area, so with my greeting completed, I stepped away and continued my work. As I did, I overheard the one who had acknowledged my greeting remark how annoying I was and that finding a few outfits wasn't rocket science.

Shake it off. It was an appropriate and balanced greeting, I coached myself.

I had a large stack of sweaters at my counter, and as I folded them, I observed the two women. It was obvious one of them was not a shopper and was clearly out of her element. She was quiet and reserved but not completely disinterested. The other was loud and opinionated about the clothing on the sales floor. They were opposites, not only in temperament but in body type as well. The vocal one was tall and thin, while her companion had a shorter, fuller figure.

They had remained exclusively in my department and accumulated quite a number of pieces. Undeterred by the earlier comment, I approached and asked, "Ladies, may I start you a fitting room and free your hands so you can continue shopping?"

Once again, the "speaker" of the two spoke up. "No, that won't be necessary. I have it under control. I am the doctor's personal assistant and will be taking care of setting up her room when she's ready. What you can do is tell me where the rooms are."

I smiled to defuse her assertive attitude and responded, "That's fine. Whatever is most convenient for you. The fitting rooms are behind us to your right."

"That's all we'll be needing from you," she added in a condescending tone, to ensure I knew my place.

Ultimately, they made their way to the fitting room, and I invited them to take any room of their choice. The doctor smiled and thanked me but her assistant ignored me. I wasn't surprised, as by now I had become accustomed to her behavior.

Other shoppers came into the department, and after assisting them at the counter with their purchases, I went into the fitting rooms to hang and sort the clothing they had tried on. The doctor's door was open. I overheard her talking to her assistant about the outfits she had tried on and the one she was wearing. The doctor was questioning their visual appeal.

The assistant loved them and said, "It's what I wear!" She let the doctor know she would be right back, as she had seen another sweater she wanted her to try on.

I had finished cleaning out the rooms and was heading back to the sales floor when the doctor stopped me and asked, "Do you like the way this looks on me?"

I was surprised she was asking my advice, but given the opportunity, I responded, "To be honest with you, Doctor, I don't believe a turtleneck sweater is your best bet. The width of the cable knit widens and adds bulk to your torso. It also gives the visual impression of a short neck and a shorter overall height. A better option, in my opinion, would be a V-neck, which elongates. As for the pants, you need a pair that provides width throughout the leg to balance your shape. This skinny look doesn't do that for you."

She looked at the pants and sweaters her assistant had selected and said, "You're right! This isn't working for me!"

At that moment, the assistant returned with the sweater. It was a chartreuse, heavy knit cable that fell to mid thigh, with pockets on each hip and large, bulky buttons as an added detail. It was obvious to me she was selecting clothing for her own taste and body type, rather than for the doctor's. When she saw I was talking with the doctor, she rudely stepped in front of me and scatted me with a wave of her manicured hand.

The doctor spoke up. "Phyllis! I asked for her opinion, and quite frankly, I agree with it. I don't like any of these things."

Phyllis gave me a cold stare and tried to redeem herself by saying, "But what about this sweater? It will look great on you. I have something similar and—"

The doctor didn't let her finish. Turning to me, she asked, "What do *you* think about this sweater?"

Phyllis shifted her gaze toward me and, with raised eyebrows, gave me a look that challenged, *I dare you.*

My coworkers and clients will tell you I never lie about a piece and always provide a reason for my opinion. I wasn't about to change simply because Phyllis was angry that I had overstepped the boundaries she had established for me. I held fast to my professional experience and knowledge and took the sweater from the doctor's hand. I directed her to turn toward the mirror and positioned the sweater against her torso to offer a visual.

"Doctor, as you can plainly see, it's too much sweater for your height and shape. The cable is so wide around the neck that it swallows you up. The color, for certain, is quite harsh and not at all flattering to your skin tone. Furthermore, this sweater is 100 percent acrylic, a fabric I'm not fond of because it wears horribly and will pill into little balls at all your friction points."

"I wear it all the time, and it doesn't do that to me," Phyllis responded in a confrontational tone.

I looked directly at her and spoke confidently, "That *is* the true nature of this fabric. It's fine for a piece you'll wear once or twice but definitely not long term. I don't recommend it. You will make a better wardrobe investment purchasing a wool, cashmere, or even a rayon mix knit. There are also some beautiful silk knits, which I really like. As basics, they will also have long-term wear and appeal. That will save you from regularly having to replace them and throwing money away."

Phyllis just about flew out of her skin and snapped, "She's a doctor, for goodness' sake. She's not worried about the money!"

The doctor looked sharply at Phyllis, stunned by her words and tone. She asked if I would choose some suitable pieces for her in a size 10. Phyllis was not happy.

I had been in the fitting room for quite some time and was concerned there would be other customers in the department, but when I stepped out, I saw no one. I was relieved, and despite the fact that Phyllis was also out on the sales floor, I stayed focused on selecting professional, comfortable, mix-and-match products for the doctor.

I returned within a few minutes, and both the doctor and Phyllis reviewed my choices. I explained my reasoning for each piece, and the doctor proceeded to try everything on.

I was confident in my selections and knew my priority was to make the doctor look and feel her best. It was clear that, while she may not know much about shopping, she understood what she did and did not like. I was confident her opinion would prevail, regardless of Phyllis's attitude.

I was tending to matters at my counter when the doctor excitedly sought me out.

"This sweater is great! Perfect! I don't feel trapped inside of it, and it's not heavy. And these pants, wow, they're really comfortable. Do you have other colors? If so, bring me every color."

I smiled, and as the doctor was turning to walk back to the fitting room, she called out, "By the way, Pat, don't worry about Phyllis. She needs to be reminded she doesn't know it all."

I gave her a wink and collected the same style pants in an assortment of colors in a size 8. When I brought them to her she commented, "I told you I was a size ten, but these are a size eight. How did you know they would fit me?"

I responded, "They have 5 percent spandex, so your body heat and physical movement will naturally relax them. The size ten would have expanded and looked oversized by the end of your work day."

She turned to Phyllis, saying, "She knows her stuff."

Phyllis blinked furiously and smiled weakly.

"Doctor, is there anything else I can get you?" I asked.

"No, this is it. You've taken care of it all. I'm going to change my clothes, and I'll be out shortly."

The doctor brought out all the clothes she wanted and placed them on my counter. I was surprised Phyllis hadn't done that for her, and it was as though she'd read my mind.

"I asked Phyllis to hang up all the clothes I tried on. I didn't want to leave them in there for you to deal with. She will bring them out when she's finished."

I smiled in appreciation and thanked her for her thoughtfulness.

The doctor continued, "You know what, Pat. You've taught me something tonight."

I stopped for a moment, slightly amused, and said, "Really, Doctor, is that right? What did I teach you?"

"Well, I hate to say it, but I've never had much respect for people in retail. I've always assumed the worst—that, well, they were aimless and lazy, just standing behind a register and letting their day slip by without doing anything of value. But tonight you corrected that and showed me something very different. When I asked for your opinion, I noticed your regard for me, not only as an individual but also as a consumer. You provided me with intelligent, knowledgeable answers, and you didn't back down when Phyllis challenged you. That displayed character, which impressed me. You impressed me. This store should be proud to have you on its sales floor."

Her words touched me deeply, and I thanked her for her candor. I took the opportunity to share with her about my Aunt Blanche and Uncle Milo in El Salvador. I told her they had owned a lingerie company and, by example, had taught me the value of hard work, customer service, and pride in work you love.

"Well, they taught you well. You've changed my mind; that's for sure."

Discerning her sincerity, I thanked her once again.

At that moment, Phyllis emerged from the fitting room with all the clothes carefully hung. Taking them from her hands, I placed them on the counter hook. It was evident she too had learned something, as her tone and body language reflected a new attitude toward me and my work.

When I finished the transaction, I carefully hung and bagged the doctor's items. I walked around the counter, and Phyllis took them from my hand.

"Ladies, it's been a pleasure serving you tonight. Doctor, enjoy your new clothing!

They smiled warmly, and as the doctor turned to walk away, she said, "Keep up the great work!"

They left my department with not only numerous shopping bags but also a properly aligned opinion of me *and* my job.

Although it had been a very quiet evening, I'd been able to demonstrate fully the passion and understanding I have for my work. I lovingly recalled my aunt and uncle and was thankful for having had such wonderful role models. Despite Phyllis's ugly behavior, I had come out on top! I had made a difference and successfully changed two opinions. Granted, it was a small victory, but it wasn't mine alone. No, I had garnered it for the millions who, like me, work in all facets of this amazing business.

Expressed Appreciation: The Kiss

I am a romantic. I mean, really, who could resist a passionate kiss with the one you love?

However, on this particular evening, one couple would bring me to a complete change of opinion on the matter.

The thirtysomething couple in my department was enthusiastically shopping and making selections. The husband encouraged his lovely wife to get whatever she wanted and to try on multiple pieces. He had an eye for style and commented on what colors would look best on her. In addition, he was entertaining their two-year-old son with books, toys, and snacks. As his wife searched for more clothing, she graciously acknowledged comments from other women shoppers who declared their envy of her husband's generosity and shopping encouragement.

I escorted her to the fitting room I had started for her, and shortly thereafter, she was modeling one outfit after another for him. He provided sincere opinions, which she genuinely seemed to appreciate. Approximately thirty minutes later, she was ready to purchase all her favorites. He packed up his son's entertainment supplies and approached my counter to pay for the clothing. The three of us chatted while I processed their transaction. Looking at them, you could tell they were crazy about each other. She tenderly rubbed his back and thanked him. He looked at her with pride, glad that she was his girl and would look beautiful in her new outfits. It was a sweet moment to witness.

Little Boy Two, however, had reached his maximum shopping capacity and was in full-blown crying mode, wanting to be held. He was picked up by his dad and three shopping bags took his place in his stroller. I thanked the couple for shopping with me and bid them farewell.

They took five steps, at most, into the main walkway of the department and turned to look at one another. She gave him a gorgeous smile and a quick kiss. He, in turn, pulled her into him. At first, those of us in their surroundings thought it was a sweet kiss of appreciation—that is, until he started to rub her back and she reciprocated. With that, the kiss went to a new level and became the start of what I'm sure was the most passionate department store kiss ever! Why, if the *Guinness Book of World Records* had such a category, this kiss would no doubt win.

You might be asking, "Why were you standing there watching them?" Well, in self-defense, I can only say it was gripping and quite unusual! I'd never seen a couple react like this after buying clothes. I thought I might have to use crowd-control tactics because I wasn't the only one watching the department store kiss turn passionate.

The couple was unaware they had an audience, although I doubt it would have stopped them! They lovingly and unashamedly caressed one another's bodies. And the kiss? It got jacked up to red hot! Using his strength, he pressed her closer into him, and I can only say their hair was in dire need of a brush. It was a mess! Lucky for them, love is blind, because they had no idea what they looked like.

I determined that, if a kiss could be measured by a department store kiss-o-meter, this kiss would have caused it to explode and shatter all the mirrors and lights in my department!

Now you may recall that Little Boy Two was in Daddy's arms, and if you thought we as bystanders were catching the kiss in all its shebang, he was right in the midst of the action! He squinted his eyes and puckered his lips as he tried to get a more focused look and imitate his parents' wild department store kiss.

By now I, formerly a confirmed romantic, was reconsidering even the slightest public displays of affection. Hand holding, quick kisses, hugs, winks, love taps, forget it! Absolutely not! Nothing like a visual to teach you a lesson! The couple's behavior had become tacky. It wasn't sweet and tender anymore. I wanted them to leave.

By now the kiss had gone on for almost two *very* long minutes. I wanted to interrupt and suggest they go upstairs to the home department, because *home* would be the best place for them to be kissing like that. Fortunately, Little Boy Two came to the rescue as his crying and fidgeting went beyond his dad's capacity for one-arm control. For once, I was extremely grateful there was a screaming child in my department.

The kiss came to a snail's finish as the couple gazed at one another and smiled weakly. Relieved, I took the opportunity to move them along and called out, "Good night, folks."

They turned, slightly dazed with passion, bid me a good evening, and walked slowly away with their screaming child and messed-up hair.

Customers who had been engrossed by the kiss erupted into animated conversation. Interestingly, the women who earlier had been praising the couple were now giving them tongue lashings. The kiss had left quite an imprint! I hastened to break up the crowd by distracting the women with some selections we had just received. Though it was a good effort on my part, the memory of the kiss had lingered and rattled their thinking.

Days later, I came back to my romantic senses and concluded, "Viva la romance!"—but please, not in my department. I'm trying to sell clothes!

If It's Meant to Be, It Will Be

I enjoy helping customers find what they are looking for when they come to my department. I will do whatever it takes to fulfill their shopping expectations. However, there are times when it appears that what we're searching for is just not meant to be found. But then the unexpected happens, and we both know that something we've been looking for is, without a doubt, meant to be theirs!

Amber Marie had been planning a baby shower for her favorite nephew and his wife. It was going to be a large family gathering, and today was the big day! Just a month earlier she had purchased her outfit, which we thought was perfect for her role as hostess and loving aunt.

I was in another department covering a lunch break, and my back was to the line of customers, so I had not seen Amber Marie at first. When she approached me, I could tell she was anxious about something.

"Oh, Pat, please, you have to help me," she said, as she took the blouse she had purchased for the shower from her bag. "I've gained weight and the blouse doesn't fit right. The front buttons are tugging and I need a size large. I tried another bra, but it didn't help. Thank goodness I modeled it for my sister last night, or I never would have known until I put it on tonight. Please, can you look and see what you can do for me? I had my heart set on wearing this!"

"I'm going to check right away to see if I have one. If not, I will try to locate it at one of our local stores and have them hold it for us," I said, attempting to calm her.

As I entered the numbers for the blouse in the computer, she expressed her disappointment at having put on so much weight. It was the perfect blouse for the occasion and had looked stunning when she had originally tried it on. I listened sympathetically as I waited for the system to pull up the location information. *Zero*! Zero in my store and likewise in the neighboring stores. I relayed the information to Amber Marie. We stood looking at one another in dismay.

"I guess I'll just wear the dress I bought a few weeks ago. It's beautiful and will work for tonight."

I agreed, but it wasn't what we wanted. I sighed and said, "Well, you never know. The computer could be wrong. I will search in back and in the fitting rooms, and if something turns up, I'll call you right away."

We both knew it was a long shot, but I gave her my word. She thanked me for my efforts as I returned the blouse and said she would keep her fingers crossed. As we said good-bye, she mentioned she was going upstairs to pick up some socks for her husband. I wished her a wonderful event, despite the disappointment.

As I watched her go up the escalator, I took a moment to reflect on the situation, but within seconds the reality of the line of customers reeled me back into place. I called out to the woman who was next in line. We greeted one another as she approached my counter, and she proceeded to tell me her purpose for coming in.

"I need to return this blouse. I bought it at another one of your stores. There's nothing wrong with it. It's just a little too much for me, and I don't think I can pull it off."

She opened her bag and reached in. Fortunately, I was leaning against the counter because I needed to brace myself. The customer was returning the same blouse Amber Marie had just returned!

"I can't believe this! What size is this?" I asked. I didn't wait for an answer as I searched for the tag. It was a size large. I had been so consumed by my initial shock that I had somewhat ignored the woman.

"Ma'am, you won't believe this. One of my customers just returned this blouse because it was too small. We looked for another one, but there was none to be found anywhere. You are returning the exact size my customer needs!"

The woman's jaw dropped, and joining in my excitement, she said, "Whoa, this is so cool. What are the chances?"

I examined the blouse, and it seemed to be in perfect condition. I promptly processed the return and told her she was going to make Amber Marie very happy. She, in turn, was glad to be part of the unexpected outcome and said she had never felt so good about returning something.

Store policy did not allow us to page customers unless it was an emergency, so I had to move quickly to catch Amber Marie while she was still upstairs. I explained the situation to my partner.

"That's just unbelievable! Quick! Go!" she said.

I thanked her and raced upstairs with the blouse.

Approximately ten minutes had passed since Amber Marie had left my counter. I went directly toward the men's socks where she'd said she would be. When I got there, I described her to the associates and asked if they had seen her. They had, but no one could tell me anything further. I asked them to please keep an eye out and notify me if they spotted her.

Our men's department is quite large, so I decided to begin in the back toward one corner and work my way through each section, starting with pajamas, suits, shirts, and then shoes and skirting back across to underwear, ties, and so on. She was nowhere to be found. In my hand was the blouse she wanted. I was feeling desperate, but a desperate mind can overlook much, so I just stopped. I needed to be still, both mentally and physically, and just breathe.

I lowered my head and looked at the blouse. Seconds passed, and I focused once again. I looked up, carefully searching the vicinity, and then I saw Amber Marie in the distance! I felt relief and excitement at the same time. I dashed across the sales floor, and when I got within a few feet, I held up the blouse and called out, "Amber Marie, look!"

She saw the blouse and her expression of absolute disbelief and wow was priceless! It suggested high-pitched screams of joy, though she was silent.

After the initial shock, she asked question after question. "Where did you find it? Is it my size? Is it in good condition? How did you find me?" She took the blouse from my hand, embraced it, and then held it out for inspection.

As I answered all her questions, we laughed at the improbability of the situation. What were the chances of the woman with the blouse and Amber Marie actually standing in the same line, within feet of one another? What were the chances that, of the approximately eighty registers in the store where returns can be made, the woman would come to mine? What were the chances that, of all the clothes we sell in the store, she would be returning the exact blouse and size we needed?

We looked at one another, and there was no doubt that Amber Marie was meant to have this blouse! We giggled as we walked to one of the registers.

"Do you want to try it on?" I asked.

"No, I don't think I can. I'm in shock. I just can't believe this. I can't believe you came up here to find me. I'm going to wear this tonight!" she responded numbly.

I rang up the blouse and carefully wrapped it in tissue paper. As I came around the counter to hand her the bag, I said, "Amber Marie, this is meant to be yours! Have a great time. You will look beautiful."

"Yes, and it's all thanks to you! This is just amazing," she responded as she hugged me in appreciation.

I breathed a sigh of relief. Mission accomplished!

It really had been an extraordinary situation. I delighted in the fact that I had been in the right place at the right time. No one could deny what had obviously occurred. Yet I'm one to expect the unexpected and watch it happen, because it does, it did, and it will again … somewhere, somehow.

Just believe!

In Search of What's Lost: Nancy's Hold

What keeps people from admitting they're wrong despite the facts? Oftentimes, accepting the truth can be difficult because it's a surrender of a preconceived idea. To admit an error, even when it's minor, can be devastating for people whose pride dominates their mind-set. When an individual is determined to fight this type of battle, I hold firmly to the truth as I know it. That was my intent the morning I assisted Nancy.

Our fitting rooms have no visible markers to designate their department location. Therefore, when we hold items for a customer, we advise the person of our department name and the time limit of twenty-four hours. We then attach a slip to the items, clearly marking them with the customer's name in large, bold writing. And we put them in a specific storage area, designated for holds, to keep them from getting misplaced.

This procedure is just about 99 percent foolproof, which leaves us with a 1 percent chance for concerns. Yes, that 1 percent can be tricky. Despite our best efforts, every once in a while, a hold will fall through the cracks and cast a shadow on our method.

You may be wondering what happens when we can't find a customer's hold. What then? Since our purpose is to sell clothes, we will offer to find the items on the sales floor. This is effective and shows goodwill, which a customer always appreciates.

Hmmm, I said "always." No, not always.

It was my first day back from a minivacation, and my entire team was working due to the holiday weekend sale. Our counter was set and ready to serve our customers. A young gal, Mimi, was working with us for the first time and catching on quite well. Things were going smoothly until she came to me asking for help.

"Pat, I can't find a customer's hold. She got mad at me when I told her it wasn't here. Please, can you help me?"

I asked Mimi what the name was.

"Nancy," she replied.

We will often tag team like this, as four eyes are better than two. Unfortunately, my two eyes didn't help the situation. There was no hold under that name. I asked Mimi to confirm the name once again.

The woman responded sharply, "I already told you once; it's Nancy. Now go find it!"

Mimi quickly returned and said, "Oh my God, she's awful. What are we going to do? She's scary!"

I told her not to worry and I approached the customer. "Nancy? Hello, my name is Pat. We haven't located your hold as of yet. I need further information from you that may help me locate it."

"*May* help you locate it?" she barked with raised eyebrows. "*No!* You *will* find my clothes. Go back and look again," she demanded, pointing to the back area as if I didn't know where to search.

Nancy attempted to get assistance from my other counter partner, who wisely responded, "There are two associates helping you at the moment. I'm certain they are doing their best to get you taken care of."

After that, Nancy settled in with me, and I continued, "Nancy, as I said, I need some information from you. Could you tell me what the items were and approximately how many you'd held? Also, do you recall the brand names? I can search our racking area. I'm certain if they were removed from the storage area, they would be ready to go back out on the sales floor."

"I had five items, two pants and three tops. I don't have time for this! What have you done with my clothes?"

"Well, that's what I'm trying to find out. Please bear with me as I search the racking area and see if I can locate them."

She insisted on following me to the back room and went through the racks along with me. As she did, her anger grew. We went through every rack and failed to find her items.

"You people are so incompetent. You can't even do a simple thing."

"Nancy, I understand your frustration and sympathize. However, we place numerous items on hold every day with no issues. I can't understand why yours isn't here, but I'm going to get to the bottom of this," I calmly responded.

It was puzzling that I could find no trace of Nancy's items on the racks. I presented the question once again, "Nancy, you're certain you placed the items on hold in this department?"

Her response provided a partial answer to the situation. "Now you listen to me. I was in *this* department yesterday, and *that* young girl"—she pointed at Mimi—"was the one who took my clothes, and now she's lost them! I'm going on a trip, and I want my clothes. Find my clothes or I'm going to call the store manager to set you straight!"

I couldn't help it. I had to gently smile. Nancy was clearly in the wrong department! Mimi had never worked with us prior to today, but I didn't want to embarrass Nancy by saying that.

"Nancy, I believe I have the solution to the problem. The fitting rooms all look the same, and I can say with a high degree of confidence that your items are in another department. I will find out where and bring them to you."

She resented my implication that she was mistaken, and her anger reached a new plateau. "How dare you call me a liar! I was in this department, and you were at that register over there. This girl, the one who lost my clothes, was here too. You need to stop blaming me and take responsibility for your incompetence. Are you the manager of this department?"

"No, I'm not, I—"

She stopped me short. "Get me the store manager," she snapped. "I demand to see the store manager! I want to tell him you don't know how to do your job."

"One moment, please," I responded.

I rang the number for the manager on duty to come to the department. It was Louis. I was relieved because Nancy appeared to be the type of individual who would accept a man's answer over a woman's. Louis, a kind soul, who was thoughtful and efficient, was new to the managerial team. He and I always worked well together in solving client concerns.

I wanted to prep him as to why I was calling, but he was at the walkway of the department, so there was no opportunity.

In the meantime, Nancy had taken the liberty of proclaiming to shoppers within the vicinity of her voice that she was receiving horrible customer service and that we were idiots.

One of my regular customers spoke up in my defense. "I come to this department because of Pat and always receive fantastic service," she said. "But then again, I don't act like you do."

Another lady added, "Me too, I love this department. The girls who work here are wonderful."

Nancy failed to appreciate their comments, and gave the women a disgusted look, along with rolling eyes.

Louis approached us both, and the gracious smile on his face quickly disappeared as Nancy began her barrage by inquiring, "Are you the store manager?"

"No, ma'am. However I am the manager in charge. My name is Louis. How may I assist you?"

She looked at me in annoyance, feeling, I'm sure, that I had let her down. "I made it clear to her that I demanded to speak to the store manager," Nancy angrily responded.

"How may I help you, ma'am?" Louis repeated.

Nancy didn't respond but rather stood looking intently at me.

After a moment, I spoke up. "Louis, this is Nancy." I very cautiously explained the situation and let him know I was going to see if I could track down her items in another area.

Despite my caution, my words were like a lighted match on gasoline, and she exploded. "She doesn't need to go to another area! My clothes were in this department, not in some other 'area,' as she calls it. I was right here yesterday, and that girl"—she again pointed at Mimi, who was shaking in her designer flats—"took my clothes and told me they would be here until today. And this woman, Pat, with the wild hair, was standing at that register when I came. They're both lying. I was definitely here yesterday!"

Louis tried to calm her and assure her that we would do a direct floor search and locate her items so she could be on her way as quickly as possible. In the meantime, I had begun calling numerous departments in search of her hold. I was able to reach two of them, but they had nothing under Nancy's name.

Louis turned to Mimi and asked if she had taken the hold, to which she nervously responded, "This is my first day working in this department. It wasn't me. I wasn't here."

Nancy shook her head in denial of Mimi's heartfelt words. "These two were both here," she insisted vehemently. "They just don't want to get in trouble for losing my clothes."

Louis turned to me, and although he didn't ask, I discerned his question. "Louis, today is my first day back from vacation. I was in Lake Tahoe yesterday."

Hearing my response, Louis raised his eyebrows as he clearly realized Nancy was, without a doubt, mistaken.

Nancy let out a disgusted grunt, choosing to reject the facts which Mimi and I had just presented and once again called us liars. It was extremely troubling to hear her maligning words against us. Furthermore, despite our best attempts to be discreet, Nancy's voice had traveled and gained an audience of shoppers who, while pretending to shop, were clearly engaged in the scenario. Unfortunately for Nancy, they weren't on her side. I'd seen one of them pump her fist when I said I was in Lake Tahoe.

I mentioned to Louis that I would be back shortly. Nancy didn't skip a beat and continued to complain as I walked away. I had been unable to reach a particular department by phone, so I decided to walk over. As I went, I received comfort amid the fire. Numerous gals approached me and said they were supportive of me. Others said they knew I would figure it out, and another simply said, "If anyone can find those clothes, it's you, Pat!"

When I got to the other department, I asked to enter their holds storage area and was told to help myself. I carefully looked through the holds and "Nancy" in large, bold letters, was the second to the last! All her items were in place—two pants and three tops. I thanked my coworkers and headed back to my department.

I was so relieved to have found Nancy's clothes. My partners and I hadn't failed on this one! We hadn't dropped the ball! I let out a deep sigh. Nancy had clearly placed her clothes on hold in the department at the far end of the store.

As I approached my area I could hear customers saying, "Look! She found them!" and "Way to go, Pat!" I gently smiled, as this was no time to gloat.

"Nancy," I happily called out to her, "here are your items! The slip verifies you put them on hold in another department yesterday afternoon at 1:21. I'm so relieved to have found them for you."

Her mouth dropped open as she looked at me in disbelief. She aggressively snatched the clothes from my hand and checked to make sure they were the right ones.

"All your things as you described are there," I gently said.

Louis was relieved and said, "Great job, Pat."

Nancy disagreed with Louis's praise and spitefully remarked, "You didn't find them in another department. You found them here! You pretended to walk over there to get them in order to trick me and try to make me look like a fool, didn't you?"

Her words were like a stinging slap, and I was shocked by their implication. I couldn't believe what I was hearing! Nancy sincerely thought I had taken her clothes on a five-minute walk to another department and then brought them back, with the intention of trying to trick her and make her look like a fool. I only wish I had time to be playing such games.

"No, Nancy, that isn't true at all," I said as I carefully pulled the slip from the hanger in her hand and presented it to her. "This paper verifies what I've said."

She adamantly shook her head in denial and pursed her lips. I was done! The evidence was there before her eyes. Despite all my efforts, she continued to berate me unmercifully. I looked at Louis, realizing it was time to walk away, and I thanked him as I did.

I went on a break, and when I returned, one of my partners said, "I made sure to ring her purchase under your number, Pat. You worked hard for that sale."

I thanked my team for standing by Mimi and me. Their support and comforting words made all the difference after Nancy had been so rude and had attempted to discredit us as individuals and as a team. I had invested substantial time in trying to assist her, and despite what people may think, when you work in a customer-centric environment,

time spent assisting a customer is never wasted time. You are doing your job, regardless of the outcome.

Perhaps like a child who becomes irritable and unreasonable without enough sleep, Nancy needed to take a nice, long nap. Hopefully, she would get a chance to do so on her trip.

I, on the other hand, went home that evening, had a good night's sleep, and awoke refreshed. When I returned to work, I was ready to greet my first customer.

"Hello! Good morning. How may I help you?"

Her sweet smile and cheery, "Good morning," assured me that the likes of Nancy were in my rearview mirror.

Little Elephant:
A Child and Toy Reunion

Developing personal relationships with my customers is extremely rewarding for me. In fact, it's one of the reasons I enjoy my work so much. These relational bonds, however, are not always formed in the typical manner—through conversations and the like. Sometimes a unique situation arises and sets the tone for a very special friendship.

Our department was featuring a big sale and shoppers were diligently shuffling through the racks, but it was one mother and her two children who captured my attention that morning. The boy, who was about three, and the girl, about five, were creatively playing with a stuffed, little, gray elephant while their mother shopped. I could tell it belonged to Big Sister, but Little Brother played with it as well. One of them would slip it in a pant leg or up a sleeve, and the other would have to find it. When Big Sister would search, she would easily find her friend, kiss its little trunk, and nuzzle her face into it. When it was Little Brother's turn, he would do the same thing. They would tickle Little Elephant and giggle joyfully. It was simple, tender play. I was intrigued at the connection they had with Little Elephant because they treated it almost as though it were a pet they dearly loved!

Time passed and I saw the mother and two children in the restroom.

Once again, Little Elephant was part of the experience. When Big Sister washed her hands, Little Elephant was shaken wildly and then had its feet wiped with a paper towel. It was evident Little Elephant was precious to her.

Later that afternoon, I began the process of recovering our sales floor. I tended to the usual tasks of sorting items left hanging in the wrong spot, refolding T-shirts, picking clothes up off the floor, and … finding a little, gray elephant under the rack! Oh no! Not Little Elephant! I tenderly picked it up and thought of Big Sister and Little Brother wondering where their friend could be. I informed my partners of my find and then went directly to the lost and found department.

I opened the office door and, without saying a word, showed Little Elephant to the girls at the front desk.

Marie saw him and said, "Oh man! The dad called about an hour ago wondering if anyone had turned it in. I told him no one had." She read my mind and continued, "And no, unfortunately, he didn't leave their number."

We all felt the disappointment. I gently placed Little Elephant on Marie's desk and went back to my department. As I walked, I hoped that somehow the children and their beloved toy would be reunited.

One morning, approximately a month after the incident, I was at my counter arranging some flyers when a young mother approached with two small children.

"Lost and found?" she asked.

"Yes, we have a lost and found department. Can I help you?"

She started out rather embarrassed, "My little girl, she had a toy stuffed animal …"

That was all she needed to say; I instantly recalled Little Elephant and recognized the two children.

"It was an elephant, wasn't it? A little, gray elephant?" I asked excitedly.

"Yes, do you have him? Do you know where he is?"

"Yes, I do! I found it and took it to the office the day you had been shopping here. Your husband had already called that afternoon, but we didn't have your phone number to call you back." I bent down to the children and asked, "Do you want to go and get your elephant with me?"

Big Sister leaped from the stroller and took my hand, while Little Brother excitedly began to jump up and down. Mother said they had cried themselves to sleep and grieved the loss of Little Elephant. She had offered to buy Big Sister a new toy, but she didn't want one. This morning, the children had pleaded with her to come back to the store and see if perhaps the elephant had been found.

As we walked to the office, the excitement was building. I held the office door open for the little family to enter.

"Hi, girls! Good news," I said, beaming. "You remember the little, gray elephant from a few weeks ago, right? Well, these two children are here to claim it!"

Marie whispered discreetly, "Pat, if it's been over a month. We throw things out. It's gone!"

"No! Please, don't tell me that, Marie. I couldn't possibly say that to these children without checking. We need to look for it," I responded desperately. "Where would it be?"

Marie rose from her desk and walked toward the back corner of the office where a big box contained all the lost and found items, carefully bagged. I motioned to the family to please stay in the entry area while I went to look for the little, gray elephant.

Together, Marie and I bent down next to the huge box, and we started our search. Everything was in black bags, so rather than open every one, we just felt the contents within each bag. Minutes passed, and I was starting to believe that Little Elephant had indeed been thrown out. What would I say to the children? I dug deep down into the box and pulled out another small bag and felt what I thought to be four short legs, two large ears, and a little trunk. I quickly ripped open the bag, and there was Little Elephant!

I walked to the open area where the family was waiting, and I gently waved Little Elephant. Once again, Little Brother began to jump up and down, but Big Sister was more reverent. She slowly walked toward me, and I knelt down with Little Elephant cupped in my hands. She looked very closely and inspected it like a new mother inspects her infant. I saw tears in her eyes, and then, slowly, a smile bloomed from her little mouth. She gently touched her precious friend's worn legs and trunk and then took it from my hands. She hugged her little elephant with loving tenderness.

Mother, who had stood back and held on to Little Brother's hand so Big Sister could have her space, was crying. She thanked me for helping them. Big Sister reached her arms out to me and gave me a hug.

I walked the little family to the office door, and we all said good-bye. I turned to Marie, and we smiled at one another. It had been a perfect reunion!

Since that day over two years ago, Big Sister and Little Brother always run up and give me a hug when they come to the department. It doesn't matter if I'm busy or not, I always make time for them and listen to their delightful adventures. Their visits are always special, especially when they bring Little Elephant to see me.

But when Mother is finished with her shopping and the time comes for them to leave, I'm always reminded of the power of gratitude and love, because they are the foundation upon which my relationship with this wonderful family has been established.

Oh, and an adorable, stuffed, little, gray elephant helped!

The Trendsetter:
A Circle among Triangles

I often wonder why it has to be so difficult to have a different look or perspective. I think of the great minds who endured the cruelties of hurtful words and actions just because they expressed themselves in a bigger, wider way that was unlike the norm. Such was the case when a trendsetter came into my department.

The young man couldn't have been more than seventeen, and he stood tall and handsome in his slender build. He was shopping with perhaps his mother or aunt and was the topic of conversation among other shoppers. I actually heard one young woman say to her companion, "What an idiot. Why would you dress like that just to come to the mall? He must be desperate for attention."

He was wearing a slim-fit, white shirt; a bright blue tie; and a black jacket. His pants matched the slim look and the color of the jacket. His blue silk socks and pointed shoes completed his stylish look. This creative teen was indeed spreading his personal style wings, and he was in complete command of his appearance.

As I observed him, I thought about his process of evolution and the hours he must have spent in front of the mirror trying on clothes to see what would work and what wouldn't. I imagined him reading trade magazines and learning until he advanced to the point of crafting a personal style that satisfied him. He definitely had a calling in the industry.

As he waited for his adult companion, I could tell he was listening to the commentary surrounding him. The critical voices were weakening him. He wasn't looking up anymore, and he seemed to shrink in confidence as time went on.

Did any of these critics stop to think that perhaps he was going to a special event after he was done shopping? Regardless, even if he was going straight home and that was simply the way he wanted to dress that day, it shouldn't have mattered!

Finally, after what must have felt like the longest twenty minutes of his young life, his companion emerged from the fitting room and was ready to purchase her merchandise. He escorted her to the counter and stood facing away from the department, his eyes looking beyond the people and place he was patiently having to tolerate. All the while, the comments continued, lacking discretion and clearly aimed at embarrassing him.

It was disturbing to watch. I couldn't understand the "why" of it all. He really looked great! His personal grooming and stylish look were head-to-toe perfect. His offense, as far as I could discern, was that he was young and, yes, unique! I felt as though I were back in high school listening to kids hacking down the one brave soul who not only wanted but also actually dared to be different, the one who was clearly a circle in the triangle peg population.

I couldn't stand it any longer. I hung the clothes I was putting away on a nearby rack, and I walked up to him. "Hi!" I said, putting my hand out.

He extended his hand in return.

I spoke firmly and just loud enough to get the attention of some of the negative voices. "Young man, I want to let you know how impressed I am by your sense of style. You are definitely a fashion setter. Don't ever let anyone make you feel like you aren't capable of wearing your own look. You're on it! You've got it! If people say things or look at you as though there is something wrong with you, it's because they're afraid to be who they want to be. You clearly aren't, and I just want to encourage you to go forward and follow what's in your heart. Don't be afraid to be you!"

His face lit up like a beacon. His stature grew erect and confident.

He smiled broadly, appreciating the words of comfort and validation. "Thank you," he responded. "That really means a lot to me. Thank you so much!"

His companion turned proudly toward me and smiled, saying, "Isn't he something?"

"Yes, ma'am, he certainly is!" I smiled and winked at him as I walked away.

The oppressive voices became silent.

If I hadn't received my wages that day, I wouldn't have cared. The brilliant smile and handshake of a talented, young man whom I had encouraged to keep looking forward was payment in itself. He was going to go places, despite the sneers and opinions of others, and I was proud to have helped him take another step closer to his destination.

The Shoes I Bought: A Timely Return

The lunch hour—it's meant to be that time of day when we pull away from the stress of our work and have a bite to eat. "That's not my *lunch hour," you might be saying. I understand. It doesn't happen that way for me every day, either. On one particular afternoon, after I'd made my personal phone calls and sent numerous texts, I decided to run a quick errand.*

Once again, I would see purpose in the order of my steps and know that to be at the right place at the right time is … priceless!

I had made the brisk walk across the mall, veering around shoppers and the vendors wanting me to sample their latest product. I entered the department store, went directly to the shoe counter, and placed my return in view of the associate, who was on the phone. She raised her index finger to acknowledge my presence. I smiled and mouthed, "Thanks. No problem."

Normally, an ample number of associates were on hand at this particular store, but not so today. I looked about and saw that many of them were with other shoppers. As the preoccupied employees passed by to retrieve shoe orders, each one politely assured me that someone would be with me shortly. I didn't mind waiting. I saw it as my moment to rest and relax, although I stayed focused and kept myself from browsing. We know what happens when we browse on our lunch hour, don't we!

The associate on the phone was a young woman in her late teens to early twenties, and she was attentively listening to the concern of the caller. Minutes passed, and I too was listening to the caller's voice. She was yelling! Something about "finding the shoes" was all I could grasp.

"Ma'am, please. No, I wasn't the one who took your shoe order. I do understand what you're saying, but my manager isn't here right now and—"

The caller cut her short and continued her verbal barrage. When customers yell, it's because, understandably, they want to be heard. But this caller was going on and on and on. The associate would nod her head and try to speak, but the woman wouldn't allow her into the conversation.

And then it happened. The caller's pitch went a few octaves higher, "Listen, you had better find my shoes, or I'm going to get you fired. You've been worthless as far as helping me is concerned."

That was all the young woman could bear. She looked at me and started to cry. I was horrified.

"Please, ma'am. *Please*, don't be so angry with me. I'm sorry. I've tried to help you the best I could," she said through sniffles.

I looked about to see if there was a manager anywhere nearby to help her take control of the call, but I saw no one.

If there is one thing I hate, it's a bully, and I had heard enough. I reached over the counter, grabbed the associate's hand, and told her to advise the customer calmly that she was going to put her on hold for a brief moment.

"Say it firmly!" I coached her.

She did as I said and then put the receiver down. Through her tears she said, "Oh my God, today is my first day here, and I have never in my life had anyone be so mean to me. She won't let me say anything, and when I try, she cuts me off."

"Honey, you've done a great job, considering the situation. But where is your manager or a department lead associate?"

"I don't know who the department lead is or if there is one. I've only been here about three hours," she said. As she continued to cry, her tears streaked her once fresh makeup.

"Okay, then this is what you are going to do. Take a deep breath and listen to me. It's imperative that you take control of this call. Breathe and don't empower her by letting her hear you cry. Did you get her name and phone number?"

"Yes, but she was screaming, and she scared me, so I don't know if it's right. I can't believe this is happening to me! I want to go home!"

"Listen to me. Time is of the essence. You are going to get back on the phone, and you're going to speak firmly, quickly, and confidently." Her wet eyes widened to the size of saucers, and fear gripped her. "Listen to me, honey. You can to do this. Now then, what's her name and number?"

She looked at the piece of paper in front of her. Her hands shaking, she said, "It's right here. Her last name is Caller."

"Fine. Don't ask for any more information and don't attempt to answer any more questions. Confirm her phone number and without giving her an opportunity to squeeze in, use the tone of your voice to take control of the call."

I looked at the girl's name tag; it read, "Sydney."

"Sydney, this is what you are going to say in a confident, professional manner. Listen to my tone. 'Mrs. Caller, this is Sydney. Thank you so much for waiting. I'm so sorry about the misplacement of your shoes. We never want our best customers upset like this. However, I'm fully confident we will do everything to make this right and resolve it to your absolute satisfaction. The moment my manager, Mr. Shoe, steps onto the sales floor, I will give him your information and thoroughly explain your concern. I'm going to confirm your phone number, 999-999-9999. If that's correct, he will call you and get this resolved as soon as he has investigated your order. Thank you for calling, and I'll be certain to pass on your urgent message the minute I see him.'"

She had stopped crying and looked at me with an expression that said, *Seriously?*

"You can do it, Sydney. Don't be afraid of her. Take a deep breath and do it."

She nodded her head, took a deep breath, picked up the receiver, and proceeded to speak to Mrs. Caller. She was like a horse at the races. The bell rang, and out she went. She was speaking with confidence, though her hands were shaking, and she was clear and effective in her words. This time, it was Sydney's turn, and Mrs. Caller didn't get a word in edgewise.

When Sydney finished, Mrs. Caller apparently felt understood, sympathized with, and assured she was going to get results. "Okay, thank you. I'll be waiting for his call," was all she said to Sydney.

A relieved Sydney hung up the phone and let out a sigh I thought would deflate her.

"Do you work here?" she asked me.

"No, honey. I just came in to return these shoes."

"Oh my God, I can't believe this! Today is my first day and it might be my last. I don't know how people can tolerate being treated like this. That was so horrible. I can't believe how you showed up just when I needed someone. Thank you for staying with me and teaching me what to say. Here, let me return your shoes."

After the return was processed, we met at the end of the counter. I gave her a hug and told her she had done great! I encouraged her to give it a few days and not let one bully chase her from a job that could possibly bring her fulfillment.

"Sydney, it's very important you follow through on everything you promised Mrs. Caller you would do," I added. "Then watch and learn from your manager as he takes over the situation."

Sydney thanked me again and promised she would do everything I had suggested.

I looked at my watch and saw I had four minutes before my lunch hour was over. I said good-bye and quickly walked back to my end of the mall. I felt a deep satisfaction knowing I had been able to help Sydney.

Funny thing, I hadn't really liked those shoes all that much when I'd bought them. Maybe I bought them because, ultimately, it was going to be all about the return!

My Lovely Dress: Wearing a Unique Accessory

Every year, Girl Scouts sell their delicious cookies to raise funds and earn their "cookie badge." I always purchase a box (Thin Mints, of course) and chat with the girls about the badges adorning their vests or sashes. These young ladies wear their accomplishments with great pride.

I have an understanding of how they feel. One spring morning, I would earn my very own "friendship badge" in a most precious way.

I had an early start, and the department was calm and quiet. I took advantage of the stillness to make certain our supplies were in order and we were ready to serve our customers. I decided to tackle some of the dust bunnies lingering on my counter, and as I sent them on their way, I heard someone call my name.

Looking up, I saw my customer, Connie. As she approached my counter, I could tell by the look on her face that something was wrong.

"Connie, are you okay? What's the matter?"

"Oh Pat, I'm so glad you're here. I need to return a dress I bought …" That was all she was able to say as she erupted in tears.

I instinctively went to her side and gently touched her arm. She turned toward me and began to sob uncontrollably on my shoulder. She was trembling and unable to speak, so I just let her have a good cry.

After a bit, she stepped back, and I reached to get her some tissues. She was emotionally spent, and I began processing her return without asking any questions. I handed her the receipt and returned to stand by her side.

Without hesitation, she shared the reason for her tears. "Ken called off our engagement over the telephone! He told me to keep the ring and that the call was the closing of our relationship. 'It's over,' he said and hung up. I just don't understand, and not knowing why he did this is driving me crazy," she said as once again she began to cry.

I felt so badly for her and could only imagine her feelings of absolute helplessness. I said what I knew to be true about her. "Connie, you are kind, smart, attractive, and loved by your family and friends. Time will hopefully provide you with an answer, but for now, please take care of yourself."

She thanked me and hugged me deeply as she left.

As the morning progressed, customers began to trickle through the department. One woman kindly complimented me on the new dress I had on. I had looked forward to wearing it that morning, as its gentle pink hue served as a reminder that spring was evolving and replacing the dark colors of winter.

Walking throughout my department, I noticed a woman carrying numerous selections and offered to start her a room. She was most appreciative, and she, too, graciously complimented my dress. I thanked her and proceeded to place her items in a fitting room. With everything carefully hung and in order, I turned to walk out, and something on my left shoulder caught my eye. I stepped in closer to the mirror and realized it was a large stain. *What in the world? Where did this come from? How did I get this on my dress?* I asked myself as I stared intently in the mirror.

Back out on the sales floor I looked about to see if perhaps I could run to the restroom adjacent to my department. I wanted to determine the nature of the stain and possibly remove it, but I couldn't leave. There were too many customers in my area. I walked to a mirror to examine the stain further.

My new dress is ruined, I thought with disappointment. My hair, being short, was of no use in covering it, and neither was my name tag. I would just have to wear the stain, whatever it was, confidently.

Throughout the morning, I continued to receive numerous compliments on my dress. Interestingly enough, no one seemed to notice the stain, and rather than draw attention to the negative, I responded with appreciation. However, my heart and mind were at serious odds with the unwelcome "accessory."

One o'clock rolled around, and I decided to assist one last customer before I went to lunch. The older woman commented not only on the dress but on the stain as well. "Why, it looks as though someone has been crying on your shoulder, dear."

Her words struck like a lightning bolt! Of course! The stain on my shoulder was Connie's broken heart, her tears.

"Oh my goodness, ma'am. You're exactly right! That's what it is! My customer this morning did indeed cry on my shoulder, just as you say," I responded, relieved to know what the stain was and how it had gotten there.

The lady sweetly continued, "You will carry her burden all day today, but not in a bad way. That's a friendship badge," she said, pointing to my shoulder. "Not many people give of themselves enough to let someone cry on their shoulder. It's a 'good' stain!" she said with a tender smile.

I thanked her for the wise and discerning words she had shared with me. As I reflected on the situation, the stain suddenly became precious to me, and with a sense of humility, I felt proud of it.

The next morning, I took the dress to the dry cleaner's. The owner, Jimmy, amazing stain buster that he is, said he was confident he could get it out.

Sure enough, two days later, when I picked up the dress, no sign of Connie's heartbreak remained.

Interestingly, I would never again see the dress in the same way. I missed the stain. The "friendship badge" would always be its invisible accessory, endearing it to me all the more. Furthermore, it served as a reminder of Connie, who chose to move from the area to heal and rebuild her life. I held out hope for her and thought of spring, the time of year when new beginnings are on the horizon.

A Little Bit of Britain
Right in My Department

Since I was seventeen years old, I've wanted to visit Great Britain. So much about the country beckons me. Its history, art, literature, and countryside are attractions that give it a top ranking on my bucket list. Whenever I've had the opportunity to meet British travelers in my department, it has always been a pleasure engaging in conversation with them. I do my best to make their visit to the store special, obliging in any way I can.

It was just about closing time on a Sunday evening when two young women approached my counter. I greeted them, and they responded in lovely British accents.

"We arrived last night from London, and as we will be in training all week, we have to get our shopping done today. We have been in your store for the last five hours, and we're quite exhausted."

"Ladies, welcome! How exciting to have you visiting with us! I can see you've had a great time."

They laughed, and one said, "Your selection and prices are fantastic. Why, just look here at these lovely wallets. We're taking them to our aunts, cousins, sisters, and mums!"

They had twelve designer wallets in all and were quite proud of their gifts.

The taller of the two, a redhead, said, "Today has been a dream come true. Everyone at home asked if, with our work schedule, we would have time to shop in America. We said we would *make* the time, and it's been a grand experience!"

She continued to converse openly with me about their work and how excited they had been to learn their employer was sending them to America. "We were absolutely thrilled! However, as much as we would like to keep shopping, the jet lag is really pressing on us."

Her rosy-cheeked, brunette companion nodded her head in agreement and added, "We must get some rest to prepare for a very intense work week."

I processed their transactions and was preparing to bag their items when the vivacious redhead asked if I had any "fancy bags" for their wallets.

"We have the standard plastic bags, but do you mean paper bags with our store name and logo on them?"

"Yes, that's right," the brunette enthusiastically confirmed. "May we have one for each wallet? Your store is very well known back home, and the bag itself will be like a collector's item and part of the gift. The clerk in the other department directed us to you because she didn't have any."

Since the gift wrap department is adjacent to my area, I speculated that, when the young women had used the term "fancy bags," they had been misunderstood. The associate must have assumed they wanted decorative gift bags.

I took the opportunity to share my lifelong dream of visiting Harrods department store in London and how disappointed I knew I would be if I didn't come home with a special souvenir. I explained that since I didn't have the "fancy bags" they wanted at my own counter, I would need to step away in search of them.

I went upstairs and found a large box containing the right bags. I counted out twelve and immediately made my way back to my counter.

When the young women saw the "fancy bags" in my hands, they were ecstatic and began to clap and jump up and down. I couldn't help but laugh at how genuinely they expressed their appreciation and excitement.

"We've been all about today, and no one has helped us as you have. You've given us a wonderful memory. Thanks so much," the petite brunette said sincerely.

I walked around the counter and handed them all of their items. They gave me a kiss on each cheek and said they hoped I would be able to visit England one day. I thanked them and asked them to think of me when they presented the wallets in the "fancy bags" to their loved ones. They promised me they would and bid me farewell.

I confess, as I watched them walk away I felt a pang of emotion. I would be in England, if only in my new friends' thoughts, the very next week. For now, that would have to do.

It turns out, the two charming young ladies weren't the only ones thinking of me from the other side of the pond.

I was working at home late one night and noticed I had a missed call and voice mail. I was surprised I hadn't heard my phone ring.

"Oh no! Who could this be?" I thought out loud. Awful, isn't it, when you get those late-night calls and your thoughts take you to a place of concern. I could tell from the number that the call wasn't from my mama's nursing home, but nonetheless I took a breath when I pressed the button to listen to the voice mail.

"Hello, Pat! It's George and Helen calling from England! How are you? Sorry about the late call and that we couldn't reach you. We'll try again another time. Look after yourself."

I relaxed and breathed a sigh of relief. Just hearing the voice of my lovely friends and clients had warmed my heart.

As I went to sleep that night, I thought back to my first encounter with George and Helen many years earlier.

I had met George and Helen when they were visiting family in California. And as with the two girls who'd come for work, their lovely accents had caused me to ask where they were from and that was the start of our delightful relationship. They would often come to the store and George, who generously spoils his Helen, would encourage her to shop. They're quite a handsome couple and charming to the core.

Before leaving to go back home after that first visit, they had come in especially to say good-bye. I told them that their stories of England had further endeared their country to my heart. I wished them a fond farewell and safe travels until their next visit.

Two years passed, and I was at my register assisting customers when I noticed a man repeatedly pacing back and forth in front of my counter. *Hmmmm, he's probably looking for his wife*, I thought to myself. A while later, I saw him standing by a clothing rack. He smiled at me, and I politely smiled back as I continued with my work.

Minutes later, and I was at my counter speaking with a coworker when I heard, "Hello! Have you forgotten us already?"

The accent triggered my memory and I knew exactly who were standing before me—George and Helen, my British friends!

I raced around the counter and gave them a hug.

"How long are you in town?" I asked.

"About two months," George responded. Helen added that we would have ample time to connect and that she wanted to look about and plan a time to come in and shop.

I let them know how glad I was to see them and how touched that they had remembered me. I apologized to George for not recognizing him earlier and teased him for his antics in trying to jar my memory. He said he wasn't quite sure what else he could have done to get my attention. I responded that had he cleared his throat and sung a chorus of "God Save the Queen," I certainly would have caught on immediately! We all laughed.

In the weeks that followed, they visited my department on numerous occasions, and we enjoyed chatting and getting to know one another better. They were an absolute delight! The visit passed all too quickly, and one day, they announced they would be returning to England but would certainly come and say good-bye beforehand.

And so it was that, a few days later, they came in with their family, with whom I had also become acquainted, and we said our good-byes. They promised to return in two years and gave me a box of delicious chocolates as a token of friendship.

As I had years earlier, I wished them safe travels and blessings until our paths crossed again. I had become quite fond of this dear couple, and I would certainly miss them.

On each of their visits George and Helen's stories of home had caused me to hear even more distinctly the call of England upon my heart—this beautiful, enchanting place across the ocean, which I've visited countless times in books and documentaries.

But tonight there was an *actual* call! It was in the form of two familiar voices with lovely accents, and I couldn't help but smile, even at 12:55 a.m.

The Perfect Skirt:
It "Swooshed" in Pink

Have you ever experienced the frustration of searching for something and, despite all your efforts, being unable to find it? You scratch your head, retrace your steps, and even say out loud, "I saw it here just a few minutes ago. Where did it go?"

One evening in my department, I would find myself in such a situation, only to discover what I had actually really needed.

I noticed the young woman searching the racks, her body language making it clear she wanted to be left alone. She was moving quickly and seemed directed in her search. However, just minutes later, I saw her come to a halt and appear uncertain, so I approached her.

"Hi, my name is Pat. Is there anything in particular I can help you find tonight?"

"Um yes, hi, um, I'm looking for a black skirt, but not anything tight or clingy."

"Oh, I have the perfect skirt for you. In fact, I have one myself, and I always receive numerous compliments when I wear it. What size can I get you?"

"I'm an extra small. I hope you have one. I tried to find something on my own but couldn't."

"No worries. They're on the other side of the department. Give me a minute."

I found the skirts, but there were no extra small sizes. I couldn't understand it. We had plenty of them! I had seen them! I pulled a small to see if that would work. But as I walked back toward her, I saw the exact skirt in an extra small—only in pink. I pulled it out, and I approached her with both selections.

"I'm sorry," I told her. "I don't seem to have the black in your size, but I do have it in this pink shade. You can try it on for the sake of the size, and if need be, I can order it for you. But before we do all that, I'm going to run to my stockroom and see if perhaps they moved them there. I'll be back in just a moment."

"Take your time," she responded as she looked slowly and carefully at the pink skirt. I could tell she was thinking about it as I went to the back.

In the stock room, I searched every rack and still I could not find anything in her size. I was frustrated. Where were those skirts? After a thorough search, I headed back to the sales floor, disappointed that I had been unsuccessful. The woman was waiting for me by the stockroom entrance door, and when she saw that my hands were empty, she smiled softly.

"I'm so sorry. I wasn't—"

She stopped me midsentence. "No, really, this pink skirt is perfect." She held it up and gently shook it.

"Are you sure? I don't want you to settle. I can call another—"

Once again, she stopped me. "Honestly, this is the skirt I'm supposed to buy!"

I was now face-to-face with her and saw the tears in her eyes. "Tomorrow is my mother's funeral. I thought black would be the 'proper' thing to wear, but it's not! When you handed me this pink skirt, I *knew* I had found what I needed. It's just perfect, and you know why? Pink was my mom's favorite color. Thank you so much."

I gave her an understanding nod and said, "I'm so sorry you've lost your mama, honey. Do you have family in the area?"

"Actually, I'm from out of town. My sister lives here, and she directed me to your store. I will be here for a few more days and then fly back home to Seattle."

"Well, I'm glad you're not going through this alone and that you will be with your family. Is there anything else you need for tomorrow? A cardigan? Anything?"

"No, I'm set."

"Then let's get you out of this store and back to your loved ones. Let me ring you at my counter."

We walked slowly toward the counter. She hadn't tried the skirt on, but we were certain it would fit her. She "swooshed" it as she walked and tenderly smiled.

"It's just so perfect," she said as she admired the skirt with a sense of awe.

As I completed the transaction, I expressed appreciation that she was happy. I walked around the counter to give her the bag, and she began to cry. I put my hand on her shoulder and stood close by her side.

"Do you want to know something?" she said through her tears.

"Yes, of course. What is it?"

"I was supposed to meet you and have you help me. You see, just like you, my mom's name was Pat, and she was a lot like you. I just feel my mom with me tonight. Thank you so much for being here and for helping me."

Now *my* eyes were tear-filled, and I hugged her deeply. "No coincidences, honey. Your mama *is* watching, and you will make her proud in this little pink skirt."

We hugged again, wiped our tears, and smiled at the beauty of the moments we had shared. She left my department confident she had found exactly what she needed and would be honoring her mama with her outfit.

I proceeded to work on the racks in my department, hanging things up and sorting out sizes. The young woman had been gone for less than five minutes when I happened to glance over at the rack with the black skirts similar to the one she had purchased in pink. There, in plain sight, was the extra small size she had needed! I walked over to the skirts and stood there in disbelief.

Oh my goodness! Where did these come from? I felt disappointed and confused at the same time. This wasn't the type of service I provided! Then right at that moment, it was as though someone tapped me, not physically but mentally, to jolt me out of my frustration. I was able to reflect on how every aspect of the sale had fallen into place.

I smiled as I straightened the skirts and realized they would meet the need of someone else searching for a little, black skirt that "swooshes" when you walk. Tonight, it had been the little, pink skirt's turn. It was in the right place at the right time and in the right size.

That's what I call a *perfect* sale!

The Yellow Balloon:
Generations Collide

Men who accompany women shopping often choose to relax in our reception area. They will engage in conversation with other men or watch TV and jokingly complain about the lack of refreshments and channel selections. Some have even said they enjoy observing the hustle and bustle of our busy department.

However, on one particular Saturday afternoon, one man's relaxation time would be imposed upon for a very unexpected and unusual task.

The man in the reception lounge seemed content as his body conformed in stillness to the process of waiting for his wife. He sat with his head down, looking at his folded hands. His personal thoughts occupied him, and the surrounding activity of the department failed to penetrate his meditative state of mind. I greeted him in a soft-spoken tone, and he responded with a smile.

I'd done numerous walkabouts, welcoming and helping customers, when I noticed a woman pushing a stroller. She was accompanied by an elderly woman, who I would learn was her mother. I said hello and chatted about our sale and various new pieces we had just received.

From within the stroller, a little girl introduced herself. "Hi! I'm Mia, and look, this is my yellow balloon. Isn't she pretty! Mommy says we will ride the merry-go-round if I'm good."

The child was so charming and engaging in her manner of conversation that I welcomed her to the department and shook her little hand. She asked me to shake Yellow Balloon's hand too, so I did the obvious and gently yanked on its pretty, purple string. Mia giggled with delight.

The women smiled in appreciation that I had played along with Mia's request. I asked how old Mia was, and they said she would be four the following month. We chatted a bit longer, and I offered my assistance, should they need anything. They thanked me and proceeded to walk through the department.

I went to check on our fitting rooms and noticed that the man was sitting in exactly the same position he'd been in fifteen minutes earlier. He wasn't dozing, as his eyes were open and blinking. He still appeared peacefully resigned to the task of waiting and was doing a grand job of it!

With the fitting rooms in order, I stepped out and noticed that Mia and her grandmother were sitting in the reception area. Mother had wanted to browse peacefully and had directed them to wait for her there. I sought her out on the sales floor to see if I could be of help. When I found her, we worked together to select numerous pieces, and I suggested I start her a room.

Shortly thereafter, she was ready to try everything on, and I began to escort the three of them to the fitting room. As the old woman pushed the stroller, little Mia called out, "Wait, Nona, wait!"

She climbed out of her stroller with Yellow Balloon and walked right up to the man who had been sitting quietly on the couch. She put her little hand on his leg and said, "I'm Mia, and this is my Yellow Balloon. That's her name too, if you want to talk to her. You need to watch her because she doesn't want to go in there. So take care of her for me!"

Into his hand, she placed the plastic weight holding down her treasured balloon and entered the fitting room with her mom and Nona, who seemed nonchalant about Mia's friendly gesture toward the man.

The man was startled to attention and completely taken by surprise. He hadn't been given the option to refuse the responsibility of babysitting Yellow Balloon. By the look on his face, I could tell there was plenty he wanted to say, but Mia's imposed obligation had left him speechless. He stared in bewilderment at Yellow Balloon as it floated two feet in the air, gently swaying with the passing movement of shoppers. He wasn't quite sure what he should do, as I'm certain he had never babysat a balloon.

He glanced at the weight holding it down and slightly wiggled it, trying to assess if, perhaps, he could just place the balloon next to him without its floating away. After a moment, his careful nature caused him to reconsider, and he tucked the weight under his leg. He stared up at the happy yellow balloon and appeared to ponder just how he had become involved in such a situation. Although he seemed nervous about his task, he projected an air of sincere responsibility toward the balloon. If you recall the beloved Walter Matthau, silent and straight-faced, you will have the perfect picture of this man. He was amusing to watch because he was clearly uncomfortable, almost embarrassed. Little Mia had been perfectly clear that he needed to keep a diligent eye on her balloon, and he was proving to take orders well!

Things began to get interesting when a little girl walking into the fitting room said, "Mommy, look at that man with the balloon! I want one!"

The mother ignored her comment. The man, however, took note, pulled the string closer to himself, and went into protective service mode! Little Mia must have heard the girl's comment because she came running out of the fitting room, which was near the entrance, and stood face-to-face with the man.

"Are you taking care of my balloon? Don't give her to anyone because she belongs to me, okay? Bye!"

Mia raced back into the fitting room without giving Yellow Balloon's protector a chance to react or respond. She not only was quick but appeared to be more direct and bold than any preschooler the man had ever seen. He shifted uncomfortably and wondered, I'm sure, what he could do to get out of this unique predicament.

Ten minutes passed, and as you might well imagine, the challenge of the task was starting to take its toll. He received quizzical stares from men who had joined him in the lounge. I'm sure they wondered what he was doing with a big, yellow balloon and no kid in sight to prove the balloon wasn't his.

A man came and sat near him with his young son. He asked, "Where did you get the balloon? My son wants one."

The older man turned, looked at him straight-faced, and declared, "You don't want to know!"

"What did he say, Daddy?" the little boy asked innocently.

"No, nothing, son. I will get you a balloon later, okay? Just be quiet. Shhh."

Shortly thereafter, another man, who felt it was his right to be a smart aleck, made the remark, "Is that to keep you being good while you wait around?"

The dutiful babysitter shifted in his seat and gave the man a long, stern stare, which declared, *I'm not amused*.

I must say I was most appreciative of his self-control. The thought of seeing bits and pieces of Yellow Balloon and her purple string scattered throughout the lounge, accompanied by a wailing Mia, wasn't conducive to my idea of a pleasant shopping environment.

Minutes later, Mia reappeared and asked, "Are you taking care of Yellow Balloon?"

She sat for five seconds at most, tugged on Yellow Balloon's purple string and said, "Bye." She was gone as quickly as she had come out.

"Is that your granddaughter?" the father of the boy asked.

The man didn't bother to look at him to respond. He just simply shook his head. Little did he know, the true test of his assigned job was about to present itself.

His wife, who was elegant and beautifully styled, came out of the fitting room and found her husband holding a large, yellow balloon with a purple string. Quite awkward, indeed! She stopped, stood absolutely still, and momentarily dropped her jaw. She appeared to have to summon the courage to ask, "Fr ... Fred? *What* is *that*? Where did you get that? Why are you holding a balloon?"

She shook her head; made a face that implied quite firmly, *I can't take you anywhere*; and moved on without waiting for a response to her questions. She asked me to find a different size for two of her selections. I obliged but couldn't help taking a peek at Fred. He knew he had some explaining to do and was clearly between a rock and a hard place. His wife didn't attempt to approach him. Obviously, it was a sensitive situation for both of them.

I returned with her desired sizes, and she was ready for me to assist her at the counter. I wanted to come to Fred's defense and explain what a sweetheart he was, but thankfully Mia and her family emerged from the fitting room just then. Her voice effectively traveled as she thanked him for taking care of Yellow Balloon. Her mom asked me to hold her selections because they were hungry and wanted to get a bite to eat. I said good-bye to Mia as she climbed into her stroller. The little group trailed off, with Yellow Balloon happily bopping up and down.

Fred approached the counter and let out a sigh. He took out his handkerchief and dabbed his forehead. I had to laugh. His wife softened and lovingly pinched his cheek saying, "Thank heavens he's a kid magnet and not a chick magnet."

I laughed and proceeded to tell her about Fred's adventure. As I described the scene, she was genuinely amused, as was Fred. He had been a great sport.

"So, Fred, will you be shopping with your wife anytime soon?" I asked.

He chuckled and said, "Oh sure, why not!"

"Well, you certainly have been a delight, and I'm quite surprised at how Mia took to you so easily."

His wife explained that kids were just naturally attracted to him, but finding him sitting there with a big, yellow balloon in his hand had been quite unexpected!

"I knew there was going to be some type of crazy explanation. Just leave it to him to get into something! It never fails!" she remarked in a humorous tone.

Fred presented his case and explained Mia was the fastest little thing he'd ever seen and he hadn't had the opportunity to refuse. I bore witness for him on that as we all continued to laugh.

With her transaction finished, I walked around the counter, handed Fred his wife's package, and said, "Here, hold on to this for a while. Take good care of it because it's called Wife's Clothes." I gave them a teasing wink.

They left happy and pleased.

An hour or so later, Mia and her family returned, and I wasn't surprised she had fallen asleep in her stroller. Yellow Balloon stood watch over her little girl, carefully tied around the stroller bar. It had been a long day!

Amid the rush of a hectic afternoon, Mia, Yellow Balloon, and Fred had made me laugh. I appreciated the boldness of childhood innocence and the gentleness of maturity. Together they had been a perfect combination, and a funny one at that!

Entourage Shopping:
Knowing When to Shop Alone

I will often encounter a woman shopping for a special event with an "entourage," a group of family and friends who accompany her to offer support and suggestions. It's my job to offer a professional balance when making suggestions and presenting product. I always strive to be thoughtful and respectful of the various opinions within the group. In general, it's a great experience for everyone involved.

However, there was one day when, despite everything I did professionally, I witnessed the absolute despair that can be created by what I call "entourage shopping."

Four women, ranging in age from their early twenties to midfifties, were in the department browsing together. I introduced myself and asked what had brought them to the store. The eldest in the group pointed to one of the women and said, "Carly is marrying my brother and shopping for her honeymoon in Hawaii."

I congratulated Carly on the wonderful news and suggested she consider some of our new beachwear selections. I knew they would look stylish and provide a romantic tone for the lovely brunette, who wore a size 6. Carly fell in love with the collection, as did the other two women—that is, until they were reeled back by the older woman, "Queen." She busied herself making faces and negative comments about the style, color, and price of each item. I immediately began to get a very bad feeling. I had dealt with her kind before and was capable of working around her, but absolutely nothing could have prepared me for what was to come.

I maintained eye contact with Carly and kept her positively focused on the clothing by creating visuals and suggesting accessories and shoes to complete the outfits. Carly was very enthusiastic and clearly engaged. Queen was also suggesting outfits, but they were not to Carly's liking. Her gentle rejections created a slow-boil fury in "Her Highness."

It was then that Queen decided to put a clamp on the situation. She pointed to her watch with an expression of shock and declared she had just remembered an appointment. She announced that Carly would have only a few minutes to make her choices. I knew exactly what she was doing, and she was aware that I was onto her. However, the other two women, the tagalongs, were confused about the sudden change of plans.

Disappointed, Carly asked to try on as many pieces as she could in the time allotted by Queen. "I'll do this quickly," she announced.

I then offered a suggestion. "Carly, since she has an appointment and this is clearly an important wardrobe selection for you, why don't I place these on a bridal hold. That way you can come back at your leisure and take all the time you need."

Queen immediately interrupted, "No, no, that won't work. She just got a new job, and she's very busy."

I looked at her and couldn't help but respond. "Oh, but I'm certain Carly would make time for this. After all, it is for her honeymoon." I turned to Carly and asked if she would prefer to have me hold her selections.

Queen spoke firmly. "No! I'm going to cancel my appointment, and we will do this today."

I maintained my composure and kept my eyes on the bride-to-be.

She turned to Queen and innocently asked, "What was the appointment? It sounded urgent. I can come back so you don't have to cancel it."

Queen commanded, "No, let's get this done."

Sweet Carly smiled and said, "It's okay, Pat. I guess I can try them on now."

As we walked to the fitting room, I overheard the tagalongs ask Queen about the appointment. She spoke of it in vague terms, and the two, once again, were left completely baffled. I focused my attention on

Carly and asked about her wedding. She had just moved to the area and knew no one except her fiancé's family and her new coworkers at a local insurance company. Her sister was going to be her maid of honor and was to fly out from Georgia, along with her parents, four days before the wedding.

I arranged Carly's selections in the fitting room. She was so excited, and as I stepped out of the room I said, "Enjoy! This is a very special time in your life. I'll be happy to help if you need size changes or anything else, okay?"

"Thank you so much, Pat. I really appreciate all you've done today. I want to look beautiful for Timothy!"

"Absolutely! We'll make sure of that!" I assured her.

As I approached the fitting room reception area, I overheard Queen speaking to the tagalongs. "When she comes out, we're going to tell her we don't like any of the outfits. Just make up reasons why she shouldn't get them. Even if you do like them, tell her you don't."

I could not believe what I had just heard! Motionless and stunned, I felt sick inside. Queen was a demon in denim, and it was obvious the tagalongs feared her.

"Okay," they responded hesitantly, with timid voices, and prepared to follow their given orders.

It took me a moment to assess the situation, but I collected myself and hoped that perhaps I could soften the hearts of the tagalongs. I put on a confident smile and walked out to the reception area.

"So, ladies, Carly's getting ready and should be out in a few minutes. She's so sweet, isn't she? It's great to see you being so supportive, especially since she's so far from family and friends. That must be hard on her. Why, if I had just moved here from another state to start a new life, I'd appreciate all the support I could get! By the way, are any of you in the wedding party?"

The tagalongs looked at one another and then at Queen and finally at me. They said nothing, evidently unable to respond.

I smiled, certain my words had made a direct hit on their consciences and quickly excused myself to help Carly.

I knocked on the fitting room door and as Carly opened it, she exclaimed, "I love this outfit!"

Without divulging what I'd heard, I began to encourage her. I told her how lovely she looked, what a romantic outfit it was, and how appealing it was going to be to her man.

"Oh, I know! He's going to love it!" she said, looking in the mirror. She excitedly turned to me and said, "I want to go out and show them how I look. Queen has offered to buy me three outfits, so I really want her opinion."

If I felt sick before, I felt even worse now. This offer from Queen was obviously a control tactic, rather than a generous, heartfelt gesture.

Carly walked out beaming. When the three of them saw her, their facial expressions gave them away. They were clearly taken aback by how lovely she looked. However, they quickly regrouped and began to dismiss the outfit. I interjected my stylist opinion, and other customers even commented on how adorable she looked, but the entourage of three silenced our suggestions and compliments. It was one of the cruelest things I had ever witnessed toward someone who so innocently wanted approval.

Carly went back into the fitting room. I did my best to comfort her and remind her of how she had felt when she first tried the piece on. Unfortunately, the disapproval of her entourage had prevailed. She was clearly disappointed they hadn't liked the outfit but was determined to try on another one. I said I was proud of her and told her not to give up. While she was changing, I stepped out and discreetly told my partners about the situation. I asked them, if they were available when Carly came out, to provide honest and supportive commentary.

Again, the same thing happened. Regardless of my words, my partners' words, and the words of perfect strangers, the three prevailed, despite the fact that Carly had loved the outfit moments earlier. She went back to her fitting room, and I decided to approach the three in a tactful, yet direct manner.

"Ladies, what's going on? Why are you telling her the outfits look awful on her and that she looks silly and overdressed? She looks lovely. Why are you doing this to her?"

The tagalongs stared dumbly at me. They turned to look at Queen and then down at their laps, unable to answer, unable to explain or justify their behavior.

Queen spoke up and tried to turn the tables on me. "What's wrong? Are you mad because you're not going to earn a commission after all the time you've spent trying to convince her to buy the clothes?"

Stepping close to her, I calmly responded, "I don't work on commission. I gain satisfaction from dressing women in clothes that make them look lovely. That's how I make money! That's how I sleep at night too, by doing right by my customers!"

She dismissed me by making an ugly face.

Carly came out shortly thereafter. This time the tagalongs were silent. One of them got up and went to the bathroom while the other sat there, tilting her head from side to side, attempting to act as if she were thinking on her own. Queen boldly declared the outfit unsuitable and added, "Coming to this store has been a waste of time."

I gently approached Carly in front of them. "Carly, what do you think of this outfit, sweetheart? You liked all of them before you came out here. You were certain your fiancé would love you in all of these."

Carly knew I was speaking the truth but felt she needed to be loyal to her soon-to-be in-laws and set her own feelings aside. "I know, Pat. I'm just going to have to think about it, I guess." Her lips quivered as she spoke in a soft, meek voice, looking down.

I offered her the option of opening her own account so she wouldn't feel tied to Queen, but Her Royal Tyrant rudely interjected. "You don't have money to be spending on ugly clothes."

I stayed focused on Carly and softly responded, "They're not ugly clothes, honey. You looked lovely in them!"

"Yeah, right!" Queen remarked in a mocking tone and once again subjected me to one of her ugly faces.

Carly surrendered to their wishes. I was so hurt for her. Queen ordered the one tagalong to go into the fitting room and help Carly hurry up because she was hungry and wanted to go to lunch. The other tagalong returned from the bathroom, her eyes and face red. She had clearly reflected on her behavior, and her heart had challenged her, but it was of no use.

I was deeply saddened and felt terrible. All my encouragement and professional advice were worthless in the face of this type of assault. Unless I wanted to start a family feud, my hands were tied.

A few minutes later, Carly and the tagalong came out of the fitting room. She sweetly thanked me and apologized for wasting my time. Queen stood up, triumphant at having successfully achieved her goal.

I took Carly's hand and said, "Honey, I wish you all the best, and no, you haven't wasted my time at all! I'm going to put these clothes on a bridal hold for you in the event you change your mind. I also suggest you show your sister and mom the clothes online and get their opinions. They love you and know you best."

I gave her a hug and encouraged her to call me if she had any questions. I handed her my card, and she bravely tried to hide her disappointment as she and the tagalongs turned to leave. It was truly a difficult and painful situation to observe.

Queen stayed just a few seconds behind; she turned and smiled wickedly at me. She obviously felt proud at having reigned over the situation. I smiled back at her, not because I was trying to be jovial but because I believe in the power of the principle that what you sow, you will reap ... one day!

Yes, as she walked away, I envisioned the legs of her throne being broken beneath her, the diamonds of her invisible crown being individually plucked out and shown to be as fake as she was, and her royal robe of pride and arrogance being replaced with one of humility.

I have revisited this event many times. It deeply impacted me, both personally and professionally, and I have continued to ask myself if I should have done something differently.

Sadly, Carly never returned to the department, and I've often wondered what transpired in her relationships with her new family. For her sake, and yes, even Queen's, I hope something positive did!

The Heirloom Bracelet: Shopping for Mama's Pajamas

My partners and I are often surprised at the costly items left behind in fitting rooms. Valuables such as phones; clothing; handbags; various types of eyeglasses; and, of course, jewelry are the most routinely found. When any of these items are discovered, we immediately register them with our lost and found department in anticipation of the rightful owner claiming their belonging.

One Saturday afternoon, I would become uniquely involved with the discovery of a beautiful heirloom bracelet.

I was at the counter assisting a customer when an older woman approached me. "Dear, I know you've been working here a long time, so I feel comfortable giving this to you. I found it on the changing room floor. I know jewelry, and *this* is an expensive bracelet," she said holding it close to my face and then firmly placing it in my hand.

"Why, thank you! I'm sure that whoever lost this will be very appreciative of your honesty. I assure you I will take it to the lost and found department just as soon as I'm done here!" I gently squeezed her arm in appreciation.

She waved her aged hand at me as though she had done nothing and said, "Well, it's just the right thing to do, now isn't it?"

"It certainly is, and I thank you for doing it!"

My customer had caught sight of the bracelet with its stunning precious stones and likewise commended the woman. "You're a very special lady. People like you give inspiration and hope in this society. You're just wonderful."

The old woman repeated the dismissive wave of her hand as she swelled with pride at being acknowledged for her honesty.

After assisting my customer, I alerted my partners of the bracelet and proceeded to the lost and found department to secure its safekeeping.

Minutes later, I returned to my counter and assisted several other customers. As time passed, I was surprised no one had come to claim the bracelet. I pondered how someone could fail to notice it missing. It was a wide bracelet with approximately four rows of precious stones. It was a stunning piece.

My lunch hour approached, and as always, I let my team know that I was off for the hour.

"Enjoy your lunch, Pat. We'll keep our eyes and ears open for the bracelet lady," they said, knowing I appreciated their diligence.

In the lunchroom, I chatted with coworkers as I ate my sandwich. We discussed the typical crowds of the day and the sales that were in effect. I remembered there were some cute lounge pajamas I wanted to buy my mama, so I finished up and headed upstairs to the lingerie department.

The area was busy with shoppers taking advantage of the great sales. I greeted the associates who were out on the sales floor and proceeded to get distracted. There were so many lovely things, and I spent a few minutes looking at whatever caught my eye. I glanced at my watch and saw that I only had about twenty-five minutes left, so I redirected my intentions and placed my focus on what I had come for, Mama's pajamas!

I found some brightly colored ones with little birds and flowers on them. I tucked them under my arm and proceeded toward the counter. Oh, oh, wait a minute; my eye caught sight of some adorable panties on sale. I veered over to take a quick look. I stood over the display and admired them.

Hmmm, need or want? I asked myself.

Do I really need these?

No! No, I don't!

Oh, but they're so nice!

Ah, but everything eventually goes on an even bigger sale, I coached myself. While I debated with the financial manager within me, I overheard Bobbi talking with her customer at the counter.

"Yes, we are very busy today, but I'm glad I was able to help you get fitted in this new bra."

The woman was most appreciative and thanked Bobbi for her expertise.

The woman, who appeared to be in her late seventies, continued, "I wonder, does your store have a lost and found department? I know it sounds silly, but I noticed my bracelet missing shortly after I was in the fitting room with you. It's an heirloom piece that my great-grandmother passed down to my grandmother, and she to my mother, and my mother to me."

Bobbi responded, "Yes, we do. It's downstairs. Why didn't you say something? I would have waited to fit you."

"Well, the truth is, I have so much jewelry that, well, I don't need it. But for the sake of its family heritage, I need to find it."

Bobbi looked at the woman with surprise, as did I. My thoughts immediately went to the bracelet I had turned in earlier.

I approached and said, "Excuse me, ma'am. Were you downstairs shopping today?"

"Yes, I was. Why?"

"Can you describe your bracelet to me?"

"Of course I can! It's a wide band with four rows of little, precious stones ..."

I smiled with excitement. "Ma'am, a woman found your bracelet on the fitting room floor. She brought it to my counter, and I in turn took it to our lost and found department. Your bracelet is safe and ready for you to claim!"

Everyone near the counter rejoiced at the news and began to comment on the situation. We were all so happy for her.

"Well, what do you know. I just can't believe this! *You* personally took my bracelet to the lost and found department?" she asked.

"Yes, I did. My name is Pat and I work in the women's department downstairs."

"Well, I'm very thankful to you!"

"It was no problem, I'm just so happy to have run into you here! It's really quite remarkable, don't you think? Especially when you consider how many people there are in the store today!"

Everyone within earshot echoed my sentiment and the woman agreed.

She collected her purchase from Bobbi, and I asked if she would like me to escort her to the office.

She looked up and, after a moment's thought, said, "Well, ummm, no! I think I will finish my shopping before I get my bracelet. I know it's in a safe place. I will only be another hour or so."

She left the lingerie department very happy. And no wonder! She had purchased a properly fitting bra, her expensive heirloom bracelet had been found, and she still had money to shop. That would make a great day for anyone.

Her actions proved her statement to Bobbi to be true. She indeed had too much jewelry. Truth was, I looked at the panties in my hand and realized I had just learned a lesson. Like the woman with her jewelry, I had more than my share of panties. I quickly put them back and then took my purchase to the counter, where Bobbi greeted me.

"Wow! That was so neat how you found that woman's bracelet. What unbelievable timing! Is this all for you today, Pat?"

"Yes, Bobbi. Just Mama's pajamas."

They had been the reason I had gone to the lingerie department in the first place.

Or at least that's what I'd thought!

My Furry "Clients": Women and Their Dogs

I will never forget the loving kindness that was shown to me when I had to put down my chihuahua, Lexi. I had taken an additional day off to recover from the grief of losing my little friend of fourteen years. When I arrived at work, I was comforted by cards and phone messages from clients expressing their thoughts of sympathy toward me. Many came in to say hello and offer a hug. We shared the common bond of loving an animal, the joy animals give as companions, and the grief we feel when we lose them.

This story offers a view of some of my four-legged "clients" and how deeply they are loved.

Hester is a mix of, well, who knows. He weighs about twelve pounds and is the shaggy companion of Millie, a widow who lives alone, without family in the area. Hester rides in a brown stroller and stays cozy with his red blanket and the stuffed pony he loves to sleep and cuddle with.

One day, I approached Millie and asked how she and Hester were doing.

"Oh, I'm fine, but Hester has been a little under the weather."

I bent down to greet Hester, and he showed his teeth and snapped at me. I quickly jumped back.

"Oh, oh dear! He really *is* under the weather. I don't think he likes me today," I declared as he growled and fixed me in his gaze.

"Oh no, Hester *loves* you, Pat," Millie said, trying to reassure me.

I didn't want to be rude, but I couldn't have disagreed more. I asked Millie to let me know if she needed anything, as I didn't want to upset Hester any further.

"That's fine, dear. Thank you! Say good-bye to Pat, Hester."

I smiled and waved good-bye, but Hester completely ignored me. He didn't even bother to slightly wag his tail, as was his custom. Considering his mood, it was just as well. I just hoped he would stay in his little stroller and not chase me down.

In hindsight, perhaps he didn't like my outfit that day.

Peanut is a reddish-brown Lhasa-Pomeranian mix. She is always perfectly groomed with a colorful, little bow on her head and a bright yellow collar. Peanut is a sweetheart and is treasured by Louisa, her "mom."

"Hi, Louisa! How are you and Peanut doing?"

Out like clockwork comes my little "client" from her designer, handheld carrier and frantically begins to lick my hand. From within the carrier, her tail thumps a good drummer's beat.

Clearly, Peanut is Louisa's pride and joy. She shares stories with me about Peanut's good attributes, as well as her misbehaviors—such as the time she took issue with Louisa's new leather heels and chewed them to bits. I try to redeem Peanut by telling Louisa that we're all entitled to a bad day once in a while. She shakes her head and tells me I'm hopeless, reminding me that little Peanut needs discipline. But when she looks into Peanut's brown eyes, it's quite obvious that *she's* the one who's hopeless. Why, I bet Peanut could chew another pair of Louisa's favorite shoes and her consequence would be ...? *Absolutely nothing!*

Ruby is a little Yorkie who belongs to Lauren. She is a gentle and precious little friend, dearly loved and celebrated! Lauren recently moved to Nevada and purchased a new wardrobe for Ruby in preparation for the snowy winters. When Lauren returned for a visit, she didn't show me pictures of her new home but rather of Ruby's birthday party celebration.

Wearing a little pink birthday hat and necklace, Ruby celebrated her sixth birthday with a puppy companion and yummy (or so I'm told) doggie cupcakes.

I laughed at how cute the pictures were, and Lauren tenderly said, "Pat, you get it! Most people think I'm crazy, but you really appreciate what I do for Ruby."

I smiled and said, "Lauren, regardless of what anyone thinks, the love you feel for your Ruby and the love she gives you in return is something that should be celebrated."

Party on, girlfriends!

Tommy is a loveable "mutt." He belongs to a tenderhearted woman named Dottie. Their bond is quite special. Tommy had once belonged to Dottie's dear friend, Jim, who had unexpectedly passed away. Jim had loved Tommy very much. When Dottie learned that his family was going to put Tommy down because they didn't want him, she boldly asked to have him. The family handed Tommy over without hesitation.

Today they live a life a mutual appreciation. Dottie rescued Tommy from death, and in return, Tommy has rescued Dottie from loneliness.

I once asked Dottie about Tommy's stroller being pink. Dottie sweetly responded by saying that Tommy doesn't mind the color of his stroller. "My little sweetheart knows I like pink better than blue, so that makes it all right."

"It certainly does," I agreed.

Tommy loves his walks *in* the stroller. To let Dottie know when he's bored and wants to go out, Tommy will hop in his stroller and bark that he's ready for an adventure.

"What about 'leash and collar' walks? Does Tommy like those too?" I asked.

"Oh no! Not at all. He gets very upset with me when I try to walk him on a leash. He loves his stroller best."

"And what does his vet say about that?" I ask.

"Oh, I don't tell him. I want Tommy to be as happy as he makes me."

The simple, yet spoiled life of a mutt can be very good.

Megan has a little fashionista puppy named Zoey. She is a black chihuahua whose painted pink nails are always attracting attention since they also have little glass jewels attached. One day, I asked Megan how she manages to keep Zoey still while she does her nails.

"Oh, that's simple. I do it while she sleeps," she responded matter-of-factly.

"What!" I asked astonished. "You paint her nails when she sleeps? Do you mean to tell me she doesn't wake up and try to escape or fidget?"

"No, not at all. She's such a sound little sleeper that she doesn't notice until she wakes up."

"Does she really notice?" I asked.

"Oh, you bet she does!" Megan confidently replied.

I didn't question just *how* she knew, but for a pup who doesn't mind wearing dresses, what's a little nail polish, more or less?

When I observe the attitudes of people toward these women, I'm struck by the harsh judgments they receive. They are labeled as unstable, weird, and pathetic. I can't understand the bitter and condescending reactions they endure simply because they love and care for their animals. I'm certain the countless dogs who are abused or waiting in shelters wouldn't object to the nail polish, the outfits, and the strollers in exchange for the love and companionship of one who cares so deeply.

I say, withhold your judgments and live and let live!

Losing Sight
Yet Seeing Clearly

I am a planner. I like to look ahead and anticipate what needs to be done, how much time it will take, the cost, and the ultimate outcome. But on this afternoon, I saw the power of confident courage when you don't fully understand or "see" the complexity of what's ahead.

A woman who appeared to be in her late sixties approached my counter, and I welcomed her. She was styled beautifully and very distinguished in manner. I observed as she thoughtfully laid each individual item she intended to purchase down on the counter.

"What a lovely blue dress, and wow, look at all these darling little outfits. There's going to be a lucky little girl dressed to the nines," I said.

"My daughter lives in Germany, and she's asked me to come and visit for a few months. She and my son-in-law just had my first grandchildren, twin girls!"

I congratulated her, and we agreed the little ones would look adorable in the tiny outfits that presently covered my counter.

"The babies are three months old, and I can't wait to see them. You see, I'm going blind. My ophthalmologist says my vision will be gone within two years at most. I selected each outfit with a special detail so I can easily memorize how my little granddaughters looked in them."

I was stung by the severity of her words. I'm a grandmother, and when I buy clothes for my little grandsons, I'm just envisioning them tumbling about and having fun. I've never thought of having to force a detail for memory's sake.

I wanted to help her and believed there must be a cure somehow, somewhere.

"I'm so sorry to hear this," I said. I didn't want to make her divulge her diagnosis, so I quickly added, "And you've gotten a second opinion, right?"

"You bet I have! At this point, I have to go forward every day and cherish everything I see. I try to take in all the beautiful colors and details of everything around me, like your curls."

Her genuine words made me smile. I tenderly wrapped each outfit and asked, "What about this beautiful blue dress? Where are you going to wear it?"

"My daughter is going to take me out to dinner when I get there. I want to look special for her."

"You will look stunning," I assured her.

I was trying to be thoughtful with my words and express sincere empathy without making her feel like a victim. "Ma'am, the outfit you're wearing today shows your attention to detail. Your look is absolutely perfect!"

She smiled in appreciation of my compliment and gently stroked the belt around her waist.

"I really admire you. Your determination to bravely go ahead of your vision loss and prepare for it is wisdom in action."

Her response was profound. "As difficult as losing my sight will be, I try to encourage myself that there will be other things I will learn to explore. I'm not losing my life; it will just be a *different* type of life, and I will adjust. I am, as you say, trying to prepare myself and receive training so I can be as self-sufficient as possible. But at the same time, I'm trying to stay in the present and appreciate everything I see."

I carefully placed her items in shopping bags, and in the five seconds it took to walk around the counter to hand them to her, feelings of sorrow flashed up within me. I stood before her and looked into her ailing eyes, and strangely, the sorrow immediately lifted. Somehow I knew everything would be all right for her. Although she was petite in stature, she was a giant in character. Peace arose from deep within me, and I felt so fortunate to have come across this amazing woman. She had taught me so much in our few moments together.

"It's been such a pleasure serving you today. What an inspiration you are! Have a wonderful trip and enjoy your precious, little granddaughters!"

She looked confidently at me and said, "Thank you, my dear. I certainly will!"

I will never forget this woman. Her eyes were failing, but she could see clearly. She didn't have time to waste looking at everything that was wrong or imperfect in her life or the lives of others. When you think about it, she was in quite a remarkable position. In facing the loss of her vision, she saw everything with appreciation and without judgment. You could say her vision was actually perfected.

Wouldn't it be great if we could all see one another and our surroundings with such humility and passion? What a difference it would make in our world!

The Day of Multiple Errors: Patricia Dodge and Me

Have you ever had one of those days when you simply could not type? Attempts to be accurate create even more mistakes, despite all your efforts. You reach a point where you just want to pack it up and call it a day. Yes, I had a day just like that. Let me explain what happened, and perhaps you will sympathize with me.

Two women approached my counter. We chatted briefly about their selections, and I explained a promotion we were offering customers.

"I have that," one of them said. "Can you sign her up?"

She assured her friend it would just take a minute, and I agreed with a wink and a smile. I typed in her general information, and after a few seconds, I asked for her verification on the screen.

"My first name only has one *t*, and you forgot the hyphen in my last name."

"Oh, I'm sorry. Let me fix that." I made the corrections and asked her to verify the information.

"Ummm, the other things are right, but I just noticed my last name is missing an *e*."

"I'm so sorry. Let me spell it as I type." I verbally spelled her first and last name. "There! I think I have it," I said in relief.

"My name is fine but now my address is wrong. It's 6445, not 64445."

"I just don't know what's wrong with me today! I'll correct that." I said the number aloud, "6445 Cedar. There you go!"

"You put Cedar Street; it's Cedar Court."

By now, I had begun to sweat. Literally!

I looked at both of them and shook my head. "Ladies, I'm so sorry. I don't know what to say. I'll get it right this time," I declared boldly and with determination, making the correction.

Four seconds passed, and she announced, "Now my e-mail is wrong!"

I'm sure you remember the Wicked Witch of the West, right? Well, I wanted to be just like her and melt into the floor. It didn't help that both customers were getting flustered with me, and rightfully so. The "minute" I had originally promised them had now expanded into three and counting. I made at least one more correction, after which I finally processed the woman's transaction.

Fortunately, when I rang her girlfriend's items everything went smoothly, but the effect of my errors had made me uncomfortable. I couldn't understand how the easiest of tasks had escalated to multiple corrections. Granted, I'm human, and we all make mistakes but not *that* many! Quite honestly, I was shaken and disappointed in myself. That certainly wasn't the level of customer service I took pride in.

I bagged the women's clothing, walked around the counter, and thanked them for their patience. They smiled weakly and more than likely thought I should take a typing class.

"I'm going on a break," I announced to my partners and went to sulk in self-pity about my performance.

Ten minutes later, I came back to the counter, and the lines were still five to six deep. I took over the register that was facing the long line.

Shake it off. It was just a freak thing, I encouraged myself. I wiggled my fingers, shook my hands, and proceeded to take the next customer.

"Hello! May I help you?"

A lovely lady with the sweetest smile came forward at my welcome. I reminded myself that the nightmare transaction was behind me. It was a new beginning!

"May I please get your phone number to get us started with your transaction?"

I typed her number, and my name, Patricia Dodge, appeared on the monitor.

Oh, wow, how did I do that? I thought to myself. *I must have somehow put my own phone number in by mistake!*

"I'm so sorry, ma'am, would you mind restating your number for me?"

The delightful lady graciously obliged. I typed with great care, or so I thought.

Good God in heaven, I said to myself. *There must be something wrong with me. I'm cracking up.* My name, Patricia Dodge, had reappeared on the screen! Thank goodness I had used my deodorant that morning because, once again, I began to sweat.

"Um, ma'am, I apologize. I seem to be having some difficulty getting your number in the system. Please, would you be so kind as to restate your phone number one last time?"

I was trying desperately to be accurate but once again Patricia Dodge, my name, came up on the screen. I wanted to—*poof*—disappear like a mist!

I immediately diagnosed myself with some type of brain dysfunction, the symptom being that my brain was unable to send messages down to my fingers. Who knew where the messages were going, but clearly it wasn't to my fingers!

I shouldn't be at work. I'm a sick woman, I thought to myself ... *Hello, earth to Pat! The customer! The customer!*

That was comforting. My mind wasn't totally shot, as it had beckoned me back to the scenario.

The charming little lady stood smiling at me.

"Ma'am, please tell me, what is your name?"

"Patricia Dodge," she said proudly.

"*What*! Are you serious? *Your* name is Patricia Dodge? *My* name is Patricia Dodge *too*!"

I instantly declared myself a medicinal "quack" and felt the burden of my misdiagnosis lift. I was so happy and relieved! My brain worked just fine and so did my fingers! I wasn't going to die!

When I explained what had happened earlier in the day, everyone within earshot of the conversation laughed. Even the women in line could not get over the coincidence of the situation. I could hear many of them talking, laughing, and conversing as though they were all high school classmates.

I completed the transaction with Patricia Dodge, and minutes later, we fondly said good-bye.

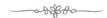

Many of the women who had witnessed the scene approached my counter with a common-thread statement, "I've made mistakes like that, and yes, I thought I was crazy too."

I didn't mind bearing the brunt of the laughs. It was actually comforting to have all these women support me by sharing about their typing shortfalls. I made numerous client friends that afternoon simply by admitting a fault and being able to laugh at myself.

When I think back to that day and how stressful it was, I can only say I was relieved that it ended humorously.

Since then, I've had the pleasure of getting to know other members of Patricia Dodge's family, and they're all as delightful as she is.

And quite frankly, I'm not surprised. They're Dodges!

I Wear It to Sell It But I'm Not Supposed to Know She Liked It

Selecting an outfit to wear every day isn't a chore for me. I enjoy putting things together with great colors and accessories. It's my goal to provide my customers with a new twist of inspiration as to how something can be worn. Those were my thoughts on the day I chose to wear the green dress. Unfortunately, my intentions weren't appreciated as much as I would have liked.

I had noticed the young couple in my department just a few days prior and welcomed them once again. "Hi, good to see you. Let me know if I can help you find anything or if you have any questions, okay?"

The young man thanked me as his partner quickly took a dress into the fitting room.

A few minutes later, they approached the counter, ready to make their purchase.

"I love this dress!" I said. "I actually have it and wore it just the other day!

The young woman ignored me, but the young man responded with innocent excitement. "We know! We were here and saw you wearing it.

My girlfriend liked how it looked on you so much that she wanted to come back and try it on. And now, see, she's buying it!"

He had no idea that a volcano was about to erupt next to him. The young woman quickly turned and gave him a furious look. She pursed her lips and angrily moved a foot away from him. He didn't understand what was going on or why she was so angry with him.

"What's the problem?" he asked.

"Why did you have to tell her we saw her wearing it, and *that* was the reason I was buying it? It's none of her business why I'm buying it."

"Are you kidding me?" he responded in surprise. "That's why we came back here. You liked the way it looked on her, and you said you wanted to try it on for yourself! What's the big deal?"

"She didn't need to know that!" she said angrily.

He and I looked at one another and then at her.

At that point I had seen enough and was becoming slightly annoyed by her behavior. *Seriously?* I asked her in my thoughts. *Do you really think a customer buying something I wear is out of the ordinary? The fact that you came back, tried the dress on, and are now buying it confirms that I wore it beautifully. That's part of my job and I do it well!*

That's what I wanted to say. Regretfully, this young woman clearly didn't understand the simplicity and reward of giving a compliment.

Her face reddened from anger as she motioned with her hand for me to speed things along.

"Any coupons?" I asked.

"*No!*" she barked.

She turned her attention to her boyfriend once again and, shaking her head, called him a stupid idiot.

"*No, I'M not,*" he said firmly.

I hung the dress in a dress bag, and she demanded that I remove it and put it in a regular bag.

"No problem," I responded casually.

She threw her credit card on the counter as if it were the dreaded card in a hand of poker. I ran it and motioned for her to sign the pad.

The young man, now clearly agitated, gave her a look that asked, *Who are you?* He was in disbelief as she stood rigid in her self-righteous anger.

In the meantime, I finished wrapping her dress in tissue and walked around the counter to hand her the bag.

She looked at me as if to say, *Don't flatter yourself because I bought a dress you were wearing.*

I looked her straight in the eye and said with a smile, "Enjoy the dress."

She made a face, as though I were beneath her, and angrily grabbed the bag from my hands.

She walked out ahead of him and he nervously turned to me and said, "I'm so sorry about all this."

"Oh, don't worry about me; she's nothing new. Good luck to you, though!" I said with concern, because I truly felt badly for him.

"Yeah, I'm going to need it."

He still wasn't exactly sure what had happened in the last few minutes, but we were both certain that a heated conversation between the two was just up ahead.

He seemed like a sincerely nice guy. It troubled me to think of a future in which his kind inclinations and natural honesty would be stifled by her sharp tongue and insecurities. It made me wish for someone better for him.

The situation had caused the sun to shine brightly on her true colors. If he didn't take this opportunity to see who she was, he would soon be carrying not only her baggage but also the ones he would acquire and fill because of her.

Astounding, isn't it, what a little green dress can do when it's worn to attract attention!

A Time for Change: Taking the First Step

Have you ever had to make a decision whether to remain within the safety of your comfort zone or embrace something entirely new and different? Oftentimes, the latter is easier said than done. One day, a woman shopping in my department would have to make such a choice. Could the risk be worth the chance for an empowering outcome?

I was out on the sales floor admiring the collection my merchandiser had just set out when a woman approached me.

"Excuse me, may I talk to you about something?"

"Why yes, of course. My name is Pat. What's yours?"

"Christy," she replied.

"It's nice to meet you, Christy. What can I do for you?

"Well, that's just it. I don't know. I come to this store a lot, and I've seen you here many times. You always look so nice and stylish. It's my fiftieth birthday this week, and I want to, you know, change my look and find some new things to wear. But I have no idea where to start. Can you help me?"

"I'd love to, Christy. Your timing is perfect. We just received some beautiful new pieces. Are you ready to shop right now, or do you prefer to make an appointment?"

"I can start right now because I'm as ready as I'll ever be," she said.

"All right then. Let's do it!"

As I began to work with Christy, I asked general questions, such as her size, color preferences, and what basics she might already have in her wardrobe that we could add to.

"Pat, I don't know my exact size or much about colors. It's been years since I've shopped, and everything in my closet is old. I mostly just wear jeans and T-shirts. But I don't want to look like that anymore."

"So we're working with a clean slate. That's great! We'll build a basic wardrobe for spring and early summer, with things you can mix and match. Then in the months to come, you can add other pieces to meet your needs. Is that okay with you?"

"Yes, absolutely!" she said.

As we began the process of selection, I let Christy know we would take numerous pieces into the fitting room, so she could get a feel for the latest fashions and determine what she liked. I asked about any time constraints we might be working with. This was going to be a big project, and I didn't want her to feel pressured by time.

"No, I'm good for time. This is the only thing I had planned for today. My husband is going to be coming back to get me. He had to pick something up at another store. I told him just to sit and wait for me on the couch over there. So we have all the time we need."

"Okay then, let's get this going!" I said.

We had spent about fifteen minutes on the sales floor when she noticed her husband sitting in the reception lounge. She stepped away to touch base with him, and I took the opportunity to start a room for her.

Within minutes, Christy and I resumed our search. We had picked out a stylish summer wrap and sweater to wear in restaurants and theaters when the air-conditioning was too cold. We also found a number of tops, some denim products she had never tried before, and a variety of pants in different styles, lengths, and colors. Christy hadn't worn a dress in a long time, and she eagerly selected a few for both day and evening. I also suggested that she be fitted for some new undergarments as a foundation for her new look. Christy was a willing client and took to heart all of my recommendations.

As we went into the fitting room, she smiled excitedly at her husband. I arranged the clothing in the room and explained that I was going to gather some accessories, such as belts, scarves, jewelry, and handbags, to complete the outfits. Christy asked a few questions as I was leaving.

I could tell she was uncertain and wanted to be careful not to make mistakes.

"Christy, it's all right to try things on any way you want to. That's how you learn what works for you. If something isn't exactly right, we'll talk about it. We'll do this together. So just have fun, relax, and enjoy the process. I'll be back shortly."

She smiled nervously and closed the door.

As I walked out onto the sales floor, I saw her husband and greeted him. I let him know that I was working with Christy and together we would create some nice outfits for her to wear.

"Yeah, I bet you will," he said rather coldly.

I continued with my accessory search but sensed a caution arise within me. When I returned minutes later, he glanced at the items in my hands and gave me a dirty look. I wasn't quite sure what to make of his behavior. Regardless, it was my job to serve Christy, and that's what I intended to do.

I knocked on the fitting room door, "Christy, it's Pat. May I come in?"

A quiet voice responded. "Yes, Pat, come in."

I opened the door and found quite a surprise. Christy hadn't touched a single piece of clothing. Everything was still hanging exactly as I had left it, and she was just sitting there.

She looked at me and said, "I'm scared. I don't know if I can do this. All these clothes are so different from what I wear now. I don't know if I could ever wear them." She broke down and started to cry. "What made me think I could look any different than I do now?" Her tears intensified to heavy sobs.

One of the challenges of my work is dealing with the ruts that women dig themselves into, ruts so deep they think they can't get out. I let Christy cry for a few seconds longer and then gently asked, "What are you afraid of, Christy? Is it really just the clothes? Or is it what the people in your life will say about your new look?"

She looked at me with sad eyes and said, "What people will say mostly. You probably think I'm stupid for thinking that way because, well, look at you—perfect hair, perfect makeup, perfect clothes. You're outgoing. I'm *none* of those things. I'm just a frumpy, ugly, soon-to-be fifty-year-old." She sobbed even more.

I took a deep breath and said, "Christy, I went through my own transformation. And yes, some people said things about me that were very unkind and untrue. But for the most part, people were supportive. Change is a process, but it *can* happen and for the better! I want you to think back to how you were talking to me just an hour ago. You said you wanted a change. What do you think would happen if you wore one of these tops out to dinner? Do you think people would laugh at you? Why if someone were to stare at you, it would be because they were admiring you. More importantly, these are pieces that you liked. You were attracted to them. Think back to the feeling that brought you into the store today. Please don't let that go! Come on, let's try some of these things on!"

Christy quietly agreed and asked me to stay with her. I assured her once again that we were in this together. She took a sip of water, dried her tears, and asked me to put together the outfits for her.

She tried on the first outfit and, once again, started to cry. "This looks so beautiful. I look stylish. But I'm nervous wearing it."

I asked her to stand for a moment and look at herself in the mirror. She could only see what she considered her flaws—her arms, her thighs, her hair color.

"Christy, stop! You mustn't do that to yourself. Tell me, what do you *like* about this outfit? What do you like about yourself *in* this outfit?"

My words brought her back to her purpose. "I love the color and how it hides my stomach. I like how it's stylish but it doesn't look like I'm trying too hard."

"I agree with all those statements. How would you feel about going out to the reception area and showing it to your husband?"

She immediately turned toward me, panic-stricken at my suggestion, and said, "No, I couldn't! I'd be too embarrassed."

"But why? Your husband is out there waiting for you. You don't think he's assuming that you're going to come out in a T-shirt like you normally wear, do you? I will go out there with you and stand close by, so you won't feel uncomfortable. Let's see what happens, okay?"

She let out an anxious sigh. I opened the door, and as we walked out, two women entering the fitting room commented on how nice she looked and what a "darling top" she was wearing.

I smiled and said, "How about that!"

She was too self-conscious to fully notice. She closed her eyes and took a deep breath as she turned the corner and stood at the doorway of the reception area.

Her husband did a double take and gently nodded his head.

"What do you think? Do you like it?" she asked timidly.

He simply nodded his head once again.

Christy knew she had overcome her first obstacle and turned to go back into the fitting room. She was satisfied and happy to have received his nod of approval. She grabbed my arm and said she wanted to try on more clothes.

"That's wonderful! I'm so proud of you. Did you also hear those women compliment you?"

Christy giggled and said, "I know, and my husband liked it too."

I touched her arm and asked, "But Christy, what about you? What do *you* think?"

She understood the meaning of my question and boldly declared, "I can do this, can't I?"

"Yes! You absolutely can."

As she tried on more pieces, her confidence grew. Shortly after her initial outfit, her husband was no longer the one to say whether the outfit was right. Christy was taking charge. It was an amazing transformation.

When she was done trying everything on, I provided options so she wouldn't feel compelled to buy everything at once. I reminded her that she could build her wardrobe over time, but she wanted it all.

When Christy emerged from the fitting room, I thought she would surely want to show her husband what she was buying, which is what many women do. But not Christy! She was on a roll. She and her husband approached the counter, and Christy was in nonstop conversation. She said that, as soon as she got home, she was going to throw out all her old clothing. She also asked me who did my hair and what cosmetics I used. She was a mini whirlwind! She had stepped out of her comfort zone and wasn't going back. As I stood watching her, I delighted in how happy she was.

It was then that her husband, a burly man who stood about six feet tall, came around to my side of the counter and, stepping into my personal space, spoke in a mocking, sharp tone.

"I can see you get really excited about selling clothes to women like my wife. With everything you added on, you're going to make a fat commission check off her, aren't you? You must just be hearing *cha-ching.*"

Christy looked at him but was so excited that she dismissed his statement.

I, however, did not and held his stare. "Sir, I regret you feel that way about what I do for a living. Let me assure you, I don't work on commission. You were right about one thing and only one thing. I do get 'excited' when I see a woman building her self-esteem by taking steps to change the way she looks and feels."

He let out a grunt and walked back around the counter to stand by his wife. He kept his eyes firmly and harshly upon me.

I maintained my focus on Christy throughout the transaction and congratulated her on the items she was purchasing. In the end, she had a total of five shopping bags filled with clothing and accessories.

As I walked around the counter to hand them the bags, her husband forcefully snatched them from my hands.

Christy walked up to me and said, "You have made all the difference for me today. I never could have done this without you. Thank you so much." She hugged me and said, "You're the best."

I appreciated her heartfelt words and watched as she and her husband walked out of the department. I exhaled a deep sigh of relief. It had been a bittersweet transaction. She was so happy, and yet her husband had been so rude to me. I sincerely had been trying to help his wife. I didn't understand his behavior, and I'd be lying if I said it wasn't hurtful.

I went back out on the sales floor to begin the process of helping another customer. Barely ten minutes had passed when I looked up and saw Christy's husband. He was alone and walking toward where I was standing. He called out, "Pat! I want to talk to you!"

I sighed and said, "Is there something wrong, sir?"

The big man stood awkwardly in front of me. He moved his hands about as he attempted to get his words out. "Um, this is really hard for me. I, um, I just want to say that I can't remember seeing Christy this happy and excited about something. She talked about you on the way out to the car and told me she had cried in the dressing room. She said you gave her a good talking to and really encouraged her. Um, I guess, um, what I'm trying to say is that I'm sorry for acting like such a jerk and treating you the way I did. I thought you were trying to take advantage of her because she didn't really know what to buy. But that wasn't the case at all. You really made my wife very happy today. I wanted to come back here to tell you that and to say I'm sorry."

Now it was his turn to let out a sigh and it was a deep one.

There before me stood a man who had reflected on his behavior and had the guts to admit he was wrong. He anxiously shifted his large frame on both feet as he awaited my response.

"Sir, what is your name?"

"Oh! Geez, I'm sorry. It's Steve."

"Well, Steve, I accept your apology. Shake?" I put my hand out to his, and he chuckled as he shook it.

"You really *are* the best, just like Christy said."

I laughed and said "Coming from you that's a huge compliment! By the way, you are taking Christy out to dinner tonight, right?"

"I guess I better, huh!"

"Yep, I think you'd better."

We both laughed as he walked away.

Christy and Steve would shop with me on several occasions before moving out of the area. Steve was always a perfect gentleman, good-natured and supportive of Christy's personal transformation.

Christy was quite proud of herself and with good reason. Her decision to yield her wardrobe to the process of change had redirected and impacted other areas of her life for the better. She would be the first to tell you that taking that first difficult step was more than worth it!

Ali and Gracie: A Girl and Her Doll

Some things, unless they're managed in a controlled environment, generally don't make a good combination. You know what I mean—oil and water, matches and fireworks, children and shopping.

Ah yes, children and shopping ...

While there are some children who can tolerate and possibly even enjoy a day of shopping, the majority cannot. Parents will attempt to use techniques to control their children and help them cope when they have to go shopping. Unfortunately, these methods are, for the most part, ineffective, and shoppers who have come to escape from their routine or stresses are impacted.

For example, children's voices have the capacity to travel, and some do so quite loudly. It's surprising that some mothers are immune to the noise coming from their child in the form of high-pitched screams and cries. Shoppers shake their heads and wonder what restrains the mother from taking control. Perhaps she is of the mind-set that, if you just ignore the misbehavior, it will certainly go away. Regretfully, all that goes away are the shoppers within the child's vicinity, who scatter to avoid the deafening noise.

Another parental method often used is the "countdown." This is heard when the adult briefly stops shopping and proceeds to count in order to redirect the child's attention from mischief. "One! Two! Three!" The child may respond briefly, but in the end, it becomes quite apparent that he or she is not in a counting mood and is ignoring the numerical game. The parent eventually becomes aware of this and stops counting at fifteen!

Some parents refuse to play "countdown." No, instead they go big and present the child with an ultimatum meant to present a consequence for inappropriate behavior.

"If you don't stop acting out, you won't go to Junior's house to play!"

"I don't care! I don't like Junior!"

This is news to the adult, as she always assumed that her little tyke and Junior played well together. After she ponders the comment for a moment, her shopping resumes and, likewise, her child's antics.

The "treat technique" is also popular and sounds yummy, right? However, some children, when they tire of the cookies, won't hesitate to throw them on the ground or even at me and my coworkers. There's nothing like cookie crumbs to add volume to my curly hair. Or how about a partially full juice box? It adds color to the "dry-clean only" blouse my counter partner is wearing! Candy wrappers, gum stuck to the mirrors, or crackers crushed on the fitting room flooring leave us scrambling for a broom or calling housekeeping to the rescue!

Some children are unknowingly quite creative in getting their adult out of the store. I recall a little one who got hold of her mother's handbag and decided she was of age to use cosmetics. The adult hadn't noticed the activity until I presented her with a tube of mascara I had found on the ground. Peeking in on the child, she let out a shocking scream at discovering her child's cosmetology skills to be quite frightening. Not to be outdone by the mother's healthy pitch, the child screamed even louder until the woman, embarrassed by her child's behavior, promptly left the department, with the child asking, "Are we leaving now? Are we going home?" The woman was too distraught to respond.

The colorful price tags on the clothing also create concerns in the department. I'm sure it's tempting for youngsters to see the tags dangling, almost as if they are calling out, asking to be torn off. Many children can't resist and take the plunge, ripping them off the clothing. The thrill is quick and dies fast for the child, but my counter partners and I are left to gather up the paper remains, which have been scattered like confetti, and to reissue the proper tagging on all the clothing.

One evening I noticed two children holding a handful of tags and continuing to remove many others. I cautiously and gently brought it to the parent's attention and was told that, if pulling tags was entertaining them, I needn't worry about it.

Why, yes! Of course!

Unattended children pull clothing off the hangers, play hide-and-seek in the fixtures and enjoy a game of tag in the department. At times, they are so busy running about, they fail to notice they just stepped on someone's foot or almost knocked Grandma off her already precarious balance.

It's not uncommon for those of us working in the department to receive complaints, even demands, to "shut the kid up" or "make them behave." It is even more disturbing when customers themselves challenge the parent of an unruly child, and an argument ensues.

All this is to say that the distraction and stress of a department being turned into a child's play area can create a sensitive scene. Truth be told, it can be very disheartening to observe, and it leaves my partners and me searching our purses for some form of pain relief.

However, in the same manner that there are combinations that don't always work well together, there are those that do—for example, milk and cookies, rain and rainbows, a bird and its song.

Oh, and there's one more. A girl and her doll!

I was at the register and overheard a conversation, but when I looked up, I saw no one. I continued to hear a sweet little voice speaking lovingly to someone. She appeared from around the corner and approached my counter.

"Please, ma'am, may I have a little shopping bag for Gracie? My mom has a big one, and Gracie would like one too."

I was so impressed by the child's mannerisms and the sincerity of her request. I went into customer service mode. "Why of course you can, honey." I smiled and walked around the counter to hand her one of our smallest bags. A beautiful smile came across her face as she thanked me.

"What's your name?" I asked.

"Ali," she replied, "and this is Gracie!"

She placed the little bag on Gracie's arm. Gracie was her precious doll! She explained to Gracie that I had given her a shopping bag for her very own. Gracie whispered into Ali's ear and told her to thank me. Ali instantly obeyed. I was struck by the "relationship."

Ali would show Gracie certain pieces of clothing and say whether Gracie liked them or not. Gracie was a fan of the color pink, which wasn't surprising since her little outfit was pink.

I noticed that Gracie's leg was bandaged with toilet paper and held in traction by an empty toilet paper roll. The roll had been creatively colored and autographed by Ali. "GET WELL SOON, GRACIE! I LOVE YOU, ALI." It had other signatures on it as well.

"Oh dear, what happened?" I asked.

Ali explained that Gracie had been injured in a fall but was getting better. "This is her first day out since her accident, and she's having fun with me," she reported, her little eyes bright.

I asked Ali how old she was. Her eyes opened wide, and she proudly announced, "Gracie and I are both seven!"

She went on to tell me that, since Gracie had her accident, she had been asking for a pet. Ali's mother had agreed to the request and said they would go to a toy shop and pick one out. I asked what kind of pet she might get. Ali wasn't sure because Gracie would have to look at them all and decide which one she liked best. I couldn't help but smile at her thoughtful response.

Ali's mother and grandmother, who had been keeping an eye on her as she and I had been conversing, winked at me and I at them. They thanked me for giving Ali the small bag. I, in turn, thanked them for shopping with us and asked them to let me know if there was anything I could do to assist them.

Ali demonstrated how lovely the combination of both innocence and creativity could be when properly permitted to flow. In observing her, I witnessed the tenderness of a child's genuine affection toward her doll. It represented what being a child was all about and softened the despair sometimes created in me by unruly children.

There was hope, and I appreciated the delightful reminder that Ali and Gracie had provided me that morning!

The Rudest of Them All: A Challenger Arises

It's a scientific fact; winter months can affect moods. Some people become depressed and withdrawn, while others become irritable and take out their pent-up winter aggressions on other people.

Such was the case on this wet, cold, windy winter morning. It was a difficult time for me personally, and I was desperately trying to hold on. My mama wasn't adjusting to her new nursing home, my little dog was sick, and I was struggling to make ends meet. Little did I know, the sun was going to shine upon me in an unexpected manner.

A woman angrily approached me, complaining that no one was at the counter closest to the door where she had entered. She threw a large bag on my counter. It slid and fell on the floor in between the service desks.

"Hurry and pick it up," she demanded. "I want to return everything and get my money back."

"Yes, ma'am," I said calmly.

She raised her voice and said, "Don't call me that! You will call me Ms. Ranter. That's my name!"

Without intending to be rude or disrespectful, but strictly from habit, I responded, "Yes, ma'am."

She smirked and, in a condescending tone, said, "No wonder you work in a place like this. You can't even follow basic instructions."

My heart had already been heavy to start with, but I could feel it being weighed down further by her harsh words and behavior. The bag, which had torn open when it had landed on the floor, contained numerous items and a large coat. I was picking them up when she came around to the center divider and said, "You make sure each one of those pieces gets put on this counter! Don't try to hide anything from me so you can return it after I leave and get the money for it. I know exactly how many things I'm returning."

"You needn't worry about that. I'm here to help you," I said.

"Shut up! I don't want to hear another word from your mouth. Just hurry up!"

I gathered all the items, placed them on the counter and began the return transactions.

"*No*! I paid more for that," she insisted.

I needed to take control of the situation in some way, or this woman was going to crush me.

"Ms. Ranter, the purchase labels and the receipt in the bag verify the amounts you paid. These *are* the correct amounts for everything you're returning today."

If it were possible for someone to emit steam from her ears, I would have seen it happen at that very moment because Ms. Ranter exploded. "What do *you* know about what I paid? That receipt is wrong. I know what I paid. You think just because my hair isn't combed and my makeup isn't perfect like yours that you're better than I am? That you're smarter than I am?"

I gently shook my head in denial of her words and behavior. Her entire face displayed an anger and fierceness I'd never seen before. She walked around the counter where I was standing and looked at my body. I thought she was going to strike me, so I stepped back. Her behavior was extremely disturbing, and I just wanted to do whatever was necessary to get her taken care of and out of the store. I noticed that an associate from another department had heard her screaming at me and caught wind of her behavior. She wisely didn't approach, but neither did she call for someone in authority to come and help me. I was on my own, or so I thought.

"Ms. Ranter, I can return all of your items according to the price the receipt confirms or, since you believe there is a discrepancy, I can call a manager—"

She angrily returned to her side of the counter and said, "I don't want to talk to you or any stupid manager. Put everything back in a bag, a bag that won't rip, and I will return them somewhere else. Now hurry up," she yelled as she pounded her fists on the counter.

Her words and behavior, along with the burdens of my personal struggles, broke me, and I started to cry.

I quickly folded all her items and turned to the counter behind me to get two shopping bags. I was startled by a woman standing there. She was impeccably dressed and stood about five feet tall. Her stance was so firm and confident that it was as though she were a statue. I felt I needed to apologize to her for making her wait.

"Ma'am, I'm sorry I've had my back to you. I'll be right with you." The words barely came out of my mouth because my lips were quivering.

The petite woman looked at me and, in a quiet, firm tone, said, "I've been standing here for a while, and I've heard everything she's said to you. Now you listen to me, and you listen good. You stop crying this minute! You're better than that. You have been very professional and courteous, and she has been nothing but rude. I want you to stop crying right now!"

Her striking green eyes reflected strength and compassion toward me, and her words were comforting, but I was still shaken.

In the meantime, the angry woman yelled, "How hard can it be for you to put things in a bag?"

The petite woman spoke up. "*You*! You are a disgusting, obnoxious woman! Shut your mouth, wait until she's finished, and then get out of this store!"

I was absolutely stunned. I thought the angry woman would come around the counter and start an argument. Instead, she glared at the little lady, who in turn stepped toward her, glared back, and scolded the woman once again. "You're a disgrace! Now get your things and get out of here."

I felt as though I were in the middle of David and Goliath's fight, just waiting for something further to unfold. I feared the angry woman was going to erupt, but instead, she grabbed her bags and walked away. When she was a few feet away, she turned and began to yell obscenities at us.

The petite lady yelled back, "Turn around and keep walking to the door!"

I stood perfectly still, astonished that this woman, a stranger, had come to my rescue and taken down the harassing bully who had made me cry. She stood proud, looked me in the eye, and said, "Don't you *ever* let someone like that make you cry again. You remember my words," she said in a gentle, nurturing tone.

I walked out from behind the counter, gave her a hug, and thanked her.

We introduced ourselves and I explained I had never experienced anything like that before. Generally, I was capable and strong in my dealings with the public, but with everything going on in my personal life, the severity of the woman's aggression had just broken me.

"Well, it happens to the best of us," she reassuringly responded.

I thanked her and asked how I could be of help to her.

"I just want to buy this shirt and pay my bill," she responded.

"Well, I will be happy to take care of that for you," I said and quickly processed her transactions.

"You know," she said, quite casually, "normally I would never come out in this kind of weather, but I'm glad I did."

"I'm glad you did too. Thank you so much for your help!"

"Now listen, don't you worry. Everything is going to be all right."

She was so genuine and sincere that I couldn't help but hug her again. As I watched her walk away, I felt so appreciative of the way she had extended herself and had my back against one of the rudest and most difficult customers I had ever dealt with.

The next time she shopped in the store, she sought me out and greeted me warmly. We visited for a bit, and I assisted her with a transaction.

Even today, years after that nasty winter day, she always has kind and encouraging words for me.

I'm sure you've heard it said that big things come in small packages, and that's definitely a suitable description for this woman. Don't ever underestimate her; she's as no-nonsense as they come. This remarkable little lady with a huge heart is now my client and dear friend, Bella!

The Bra:
Making Room for a Perfect Fit

I'm sure you've heard the expression, "It's what's on the inside that counts." It's generally spoken in regard to character, but for the sake of this story, it will relate to that wonderful undergarment we call the bra. Archeologists have discovered that its existence dates back to the 1400s. Its general purpose is to support the breast and provide lift, form, and visual appeal. The bra has weathered many storms, but it's still here, and its sales generate billions every year.

Now you may not think of a bra as a garment that creates emotional and psychological responses, but that's exactly what happened when two women visited my department.

I had spent nearly two hours with my client that morning. We had found a beautiful selection of sweaters, and she was looking forward to wearing them on her upcoming weekend getaway with her husband.

"So, Claire, you have all these great sweaters, but you need to get a new bra to finish the look."

She reacted to my statement with a look of surprise.

"But I just bought this bra! I spent over a hundred dollars on two of them," she said, assuming the price she'd paid evidenced their appeal.

"Claire, with all due respect, I hope you saved the receipt. This bra doesn't give you a proper fit. You are bulging over the sides and in the cups."

"Well, I thought the 'bulge,' as you call it, made me look sexy."

"Claire, proper fit is sexy. If you want sexy, there are bras that will give you lift. Your breasts are smashed in there! Why, just look in the mirror!"

She did, and the miniwar began.

"I like the way I look. I don't want to spend money on new bras. I want to spend money on these clothes right here. I'll think about it, okay?" she said with a smile, hoping that would get her off my pet peeve hook.

"Listen to me," I pleaded. "Since when have I ever been this adamant with you? You need to wear a different bra with these sweaters. It will just take a few minutes, and you can try the bras on with the sweaters and *see* the difference! I promise it will be worth it. Our fitter will make you look amazing in these," I said pointing to the sweaters on the fitting room bench. "You know I don't work on commission, so I have nothing to gain from saying all this to you. You can spend four hundred dollars on all these pieces, but you won't look your absolute best. Please, won't you trust me on this?"

She could tell I was set in my conviction. "Ughhh, fine, okay. Is the woman up there? This had better be worth it, Pat!" she said.

I collected the clothing and said, "I'll ring this up and call upstairs to have Tina help you with your fitting. Let's go."

Ahhhh, I could hear the brassiere choir singing! I felt like I had gone a few rounds in the ring, and I was exhausted. As I watched Claire go up the escalator, I hoped Tina wouldn't let my words fall to the ground.

"Ladies," I announced to my coworkers, "I'm going to lunch."

I returned an hour later, and my partner said, "Oh, Pat, you just missed your customer, Claire. She said to tell you that you were right! Tina fit her in some new bras, and she loved the way she looked. She also said she was sorry for giving you such a bad time and to thank you."

I sighed. Now I could say it had been a successful morning.

Two days later, Claire came back to the store. "Pat!" she called out loudly and extended her arms to me. "I am so embarrassed for how I acted the other day. I just had to come back and thank you for what you did for me. My husband wanted me to thank you too. I tried on the sweaters for him that night, and he took me out to dinner! He couldn't keep his hands off me. He had a smile on his face all night. He flirted with me and told me I looked 'hot.' Pat, he hasn't said that to me in ages!" She had tears in her eyes. "I want to apologize for putting up such a fight. I should know better! You and Tina are truly wonderful at what you do."

Her heart was on her sleeve. I wished her a fantastic getaway and told her to delight in the loving attention of her husband. She enthusiastically nodded as she left with her self-confidence at a new high.

Nice ending for Claire, but my work is never done.

Laurie had come to the store looking for a sexy top to wear to her husband's high school reunion. She was conservative and didn't normally wear "sexy" clothing outside of her bedroom, but she was wanting to step out a little bit. Laurie's daughter, Brooke, was shopping with her and eager for me to help her mom. That in itself was unusual, although refreshing. Most daughters believe they are the only ones entitled to be their mom's personal shopper and that any suggestion from an outsider holds no merit.

The three of us chatted about what Laurie might be looking for. I explained that looking sexy, in my opinion, didn't necessarily mean showing cleavage or lots of skin. I had some nice options on my sales floor that I wanted to show her, but first I wanted to discuss the events taking place at the reunion so she would have the appropriate clothing.

With information in hand, I searched my floor and selected numerous pieces for her. As I led her to the fitting room, she asked, "Would you mind standing outside the door as I try things on? This is an entirely new look for me."

I assured her that I would gladly wait, and within minutes she began to comment on how it was going and flung open the fitting room door.

"I love this!" she beamed. "I look so beautiful! My husband is going to love me in this! I never would have picked something like this to wear. *Never!*" she said in surprised elation.

I wanted to join in her excitement but there was one detail holding me back—her breasts! They were practically at her waist!

Both she and Brooke could tell I wasn't completely onboard, and Laurie asked my opinion.

"I like the top, Laurie, I really do, but would you mind terribly if I got you a different size—a size eight—and then may I provide you with a visual?"

Her eyes widened, as did her daughter's. "A size eight? I don't wear an eight! Do you think I could fit into a size eight?" she asked sincerely.

"Let's try and see," I said with a smile and went to find the size.

I could hear Laurie and Brooke giggling and chatting up the fact that she was going to try on a smaller size. They were quite charming in their excitement.

I promptly returned and gently knocked, "It's me. May I come in?"

Laurie eagerly opened the door. She tried on the smaller size and wasn't as comfortable as she would like to be. No, she was definitely not as comfortable as she had been in the size 10. She was making a face!

"Laurie, may I show you that visual I told you about?"

"Sure, what is it?" she asked looking about.

"Laurie, it's on you. May I?" I stood behind her and firmly pulled up her bra straps so that her breasts lifted at least two inches. I asked if I could refasten the bra hooks, and with that done, I said, "*This* is how you're supposed to look."

Laurie's blue eyes opened wide! Brooke's did the same as she blurted out in surprise, "Oh my gosh, Mom!" They started to laugh because they couldn't believe what they were seeing.

"Do you realize what's going on here?" I asked. "Not only are you wearing the wrong size bra, but, with the right fit, more than likely you will be able to wear a smaller size in tops!"

They stared at her reflection in amazement, as though I had just performed a magic trick. Now they could fully understand the potential of a properly fitting bra. Laurie smiled, and Brooke squeezed her arm. "Wow, Mom! Look at you!"

"Laurie, may I call the lingerie consultant upstairs and let her know you would like to get fitted for a new bra?"

"*Yes*," she responded without hesitation and laughed with nervous excitement.

As I went to my counter to make the call, she finished trying on the rest of the selections. Laurie purchased three new tops that were unlike anything she had in her closet.

"Pat, I can't thank you enough. I was really nervous about going to this reunion, but not anymore. I really like how I'm going to look, and I don't have to bare all to look beautiful!"

As she was leaving to go upstairs, Brooke asked if she could get a fitting too.

"Absolutely. Make it a family affair. They will be happy to take care of both of you!"

Laurie left my department eager to look better and with a newfound confidence in her style expression. I was happy to have made a difference, but it was only possible because she had been willing. She had taken the first step to a great time at the reunion.

So, there you have it—two women made room for reevaluation and now look remarkably better because of it!

Is it your turn?

Alive and Well:
A Senior Romance

The aging process is a funny thing. As we get older, things start to ache a little here and there, but for the most part we're actively living life. Staying mentally sharp is a priority for those who say they don't feel as though they've aged. The same enthusiasm goes for matters of the heart. There's a ridiculous misconception that love chills as we enter our golden years. The truth is, for many, this is the time when love truly awakens because there's a deeper appreciation for what matters.

One evening, this romantic would have the delightful experience of witnessing the loving tenderness of an elderly couple.

They strolled into the department and went directly to the clearance merchandise racks. As she reviewed each piece of clothing, he stood lovingly next to her until she suggested he go and sit on the reception area couch. She was concerned it would be a while and didn't want him to tire. He dutifully sat down but kept his eye on her.

I approached and asked, "Ma'am, is there something specific you're looking for? Perhaps I can save you some time and direct you."

"I'm looking for a size 10 dress, but I'm not seeing any dresses here. Do they not make dresses anymore?"

I couldn't help but giggle and assured her that, yes, we did have some lovely dresses, but they were on the other side of the walkway. I escorted her there and pulled a classic wrap dress, which immediately appealed to her.

"Oh, I really like this one," she said, admiring the detail of the design. "May I try it on?"

"Yes, of course, but would you like to select at least one other in the event this particular one doesn't work out?"

"You're right! I just got excited because this one is so pretty. I sure hope it works, but yes, why don't you show me some more."

I found two other dresses I thought would be appealing. She gave them a quick glance and said, "That's all, dear. I'd like to try them on now."

She took the dresses from my hand, explaining that she wanted to show them to her husband.

As he watched her come close, he smiled and nodded his head in approval.

Turning to go into the fitting room, she said, "I'll come out and show you how they look, so stay here."

"Oh, I will," he assured her.

This couple, who I assumed to be in their early eighties or so, had a calm connection. I clearly perceived that they liked as well as loved each other. They cared about one another's opinion and were thoughtful companions. I was certain that, if she would have kept shopping, he wouldn't have minded, so long as she was happy.

I went to my counter and assisted other customers, and during one transaction, I saw her come out wearing the first dress I had shown her. I could hear her explaining to him why she liked it, and he readily agreed.

Then, in a quick second of time, there was an exchange between them. Their eyes met, he gave her a "look," and she seemed to weaken in her facial expression. She smiled shyly, almost embarrassed that he had looked at her "that way" in public.

She quickly refocused and announced, "I'm going to get this one."

"It's the right pick," he responded.

She brought the dress out to him a few minutes later and asked him to please pay for it, as she needed to use the restroom. "I'll be right back," she assured him.

He slowly stood and approached my counter, at which point it seemed as if everyone in the department had vanished, and just he and I were there.

"Sir, I thought this dress looked lovely on your wife. What did you think?"

He looked me in the eye and, with a charming, sly smile, chuckled and said, "It looked great. She has the best legs—*the best everything*!"

I had to consciously hold my mouth shut, as his words made it want to drop wide open. I blushed. I thought to myself, "Wow! He is still madly in love with her in every way." It was genuinely romantic.

She returned to the counter just as I was finishing the transaction and wrapping her dress. She thanked me for my help and then turned her attention toward him. She carefully watched as he put his credit card and license back in his wallet. It was plain to see she loved and respected him. With everything tucked safely away, he gave her a quick wink and smiled. He adored her.

I felt almost as though I were intruding, watching their expressions of love and affection. As I walked around the counter to hand them their bag, I thanked them for shopping with me and wished them a pleasant evening. They smiled warmly and took the bag from my hand. Turning to walk away they instinctively reached out for one another and strolled out of the department hand in hand. It made my heart melt.

Love, indeed, lives quite well in the hearts of those who welcome it, no matter how old they are! Age isn't a barrier, but unwillingness is. After seeing those two, who could resist letting love in? Not this romantic; that's for sure.

Undeterred Shoppers:
They Keep Going and Going

Undeterred shoppers! Nothing stops them or gets in their way. And while undeterred individuals may be considered noble in their pursuit, on one particular weekend, I would emphatically disagree.

I was at my register assisting a customer when a woman approached and said, "I wanted to let you know that a woman just collapsed on the bathroom floor. I don't know what could be wrong, but I thought I should make you aware."

I immediately contacted our office. They would make the necessary emergency calls and send assistance and crowd control. Within minutes, the paramedics arrived. It appeared the woman needed further treatment and would be transported to the hospital. As she was being wheeled out, I recognized her from earlier that morning. She was white as a ghost and trembling. A thought came to me. *Poor thing! She won't be back for the clothes she put on hold this morning.*

Later that afternoon, I was in the fitting room area sorting clothes when a woman tapped my shoulder.

"Hi. You probably don't remember me. I put some clothes on hold this morning. My name is Mary."

I looked closely at her and thought I must be mistaken. She had a strong resemblance to the woman who had been wheeled out by the paramedics! "Mary? Was that you who collapsed in the bathroom earlier?"

"Oh, dear! You recognized me? Yes, that was me," she said, somewhat embarrassed.

"What are you doing here?" I asked, frankly surprised to see her standing in front of me.

"Well, I'm feeling better now. When I was at the hospital, I was hoping you still had my clothes. I'm going on a trip next week, and I spent so much time finding those things. I was worried they would be put back. Tell me, do you still have them? I want to try them on."

The thought of her lying in a hospital bed worrying about clothes rather than her health perplexed me. But I reassured her, "Yes, I'm certain we do. However, considering what you've been through, I can extend the hold for a few days. Please, don't worry any further. Go home and rest. Trying everything on now will tire you and be a stress to your body."

She shook her head and dismissed my suggestion. "That's so sweet of you, but no, really, I'm fine!"

I could tell just by looking at her that wasn't true. She continued to try to persuade me to believe her. It wasn't my place to stop her from doing what she wanted, and since she was determined to try on her clothes, I pulled them from the storage closet and arranged them in a fitting room.

I anxiously checked on her twice, and each time, she said she was fine.

However, twenty minutes later she came out and said, "I'm not feeling very well. Please, can you ring me up right away. I'm worried I may faint again."

I became very concerned because she looked even worse than she had before, and I, too, feared a repeat collapse. Quickly, I did as she'd asked and was done within a few minutes. She thanked me and commented that perhaps she should have listened to me but that shopping had been the priority of her day.

I was curious and asked how she got back to the store from the hospital, since she had been taken by ambulance.

"Oh, my friend picked me up and then dropped me off."

Mary was very pale and leaning heavily against the counter. I seriously questioned whether she should drive home. I asked if she would permit me to call someone to pick her up or even allow me to take her myself. She firmly refused and left.

Mary was clearly ignoring her body's signals. The fact was, if she didn't take care of herself, she wasn't going to make her trip.

The situation left me feeling exasperated and somewhat helpless. But given the volume of shoppers on this busy weekend, the ones I had already tended to and the ones still to come, I thought it best to simply let it go. And wisely so, because unbeknownst to me, the very next day, I would become involved in yet another unusual situation with a pair of undeterred shoppers.

It was Sunday evening, and most of the shoppers had gone home. I welcomed the slower pace, since the department had been heavily shopped all weekend, and I was closing alone.

A man holding a little girl, perhaps a year old, approached our fitting rooms. He stood at the entry and urgently called out to someone inside. He appeared distressed and kept looking at the little girl. A woman I presumed to be his wife came out, and they began to talk. They were communicating in a foreign language, and their conversation quickly turned to arguing. After a few moments, they were outright yelling.

She was holding a dress, which she threw on a chair. She grabbed the little girl out of his arms and began to shake her. Then she seemed to be attempting to pry open the mouth of the child with her fingers. The little one was crying and obviously alarmed by her screaming parents.

The father took his turn. He grabbed the child out of the mother's arms and attempted to look in her mouth by holding her up over his head, shaking her and commanding her to open her mouth. It appeared his method was having a better result, not due to his technique, but because she was screaming in terror at what was being done to her.

Since this was happening in our reception area, just a few feet from where I was standing, I approached to see if there was something I could do.

"Sir, ma'am, may I help you?"

"He was supposed to be watching her, and she swallowed a button!" the woman yelled in response to my question.

Standing only a few inches away, the man turned to me in self-defense and, in a voice louder than hers, screamed, *"I was standing right over her. She was sitting on the floor over by that rack, and I noticed she put something in her mouth. I tried to get it out, but she had already swallowed it! It's inside her stomach!"*

"Sir, are you sure it was a button?"

"Yes, I had seen the button on the floor. It was a small one, but I didn't think she would take it, put it in her mouth, and swallow it!"

His carelessness about the button further enraged the mother. She slapped him on the back and continued to yell even louder than before.

I spoke in a gentle, quiet tone, not only to get them to lower their own voices but also to calm the little girl.

"Please, both of you need to stop yelling! You're frightening your little girl, and I'm trying to help you. Is she having difficulty breathing or swallowing?"

He held the child out at arm's length, her little limbs dangling, and the parents determined she was having neither of those issues. Her coloring didn't seem affected, apart from crying, and there didn't appear to be an obstruction.

The couple appeared relieved after their physical assessment. They had another heated verbal exchange, and the mother hastily turned away from her husband and went back into the fitting room to finish trying on her clothes.

Ten minutes later she emerged and threw a multicolored dress at her husband and demanded he buy it! He promptly obeyed.

Meanwhile, the child was recovering from the incident and appeared to be settling down. She was drinking her bottle and enjoying the nourishment and comfort it provided. It appeared to me that she had experienced more of an impact from her parents' behavior than from presumably swallowing a button.

The father approached my counter and, displaying multiple coupons, asked which would give him the best savings.

I selected the best offer, and he questioned in a very rude, aggressive tone whether I was "absolutely certain" I was saving him the most money.

I looked intently at him and said I was.

Again, he asked the same question, using the same tone and adding a stern facial expression to match. "You're absolutely certain?"

I placed my calculator in front of him so he could confirm my math. He pushed it away and told me to hurry up because they needed to get home to tend to their daughter.

I rang up the transaction and bagged the dress. I was about to walk it around the counter when he snatched it from my hand. His behavior toward me was disturbing, to say the least.

The little girl was now comfortably resting in her stroller, and her parents hurriedly left the department in bitter silence.

Minutes later, the final closing announcement came over the loudspeaker. That sale had marked the end of my work week.

Driving home that night, I reflected on the weekend's undeterred shoppers. I had done my best to extend concern and assistance to each of them, but their actions had left me with unsettled emotions. Each of them had been determined to finish shopping and would have to deal with the consequences for having done so.

All I could do was shake my head and be thankful nothing more serious had ensued under either circumstance. Thankfully, it was all behind me, and I breathed a sigh of relief as I pulled into my driveway.

Home has a way of making everything all right!

A Customer Lesson:
Insurance Is a Good Thing

In my line of work, listening is very important. On one Sunday evening, when I was feeling a bit out of sorts, I heard something so loud and clear that it snapped me right back into proper perspective.

Truth be told, I was irritated and in a complaining kind of mood. What about? My homeowner's insurance! It was obvious I had to be responsible and get coverage, but I didn't want to fall into the worrywart trap and go overboard. In the end, to my agent's credit, my coverage was sufficient and affordable.

Yet I still felt miserable about the cost. *Get over it and be thankful you own a place to insure*, I chided myself. I shot an arrow prayer. *Help! I need an attitude adjustment.*

I hit the target with that arrow because the answer arrived within a minute in the form of a petite brunette who approached my counter.

"Hi. How are you tonight?" I asked.

"Oh, I'm just so happy. These are the first clothes that I've been able to buy since my duplex caught on fire a week ago."

I looked down at the three crew neck T-shirts she was purchasing and asked, "Honey, what happened?"

"It was just awful. I lost everything, and I mean *everything!* Nothing was left! You have no idea how wonderful it's going to feel to wear something other than these clothes."

Wait a minute! How could it be that she had been wearing the same clothes for a week? Didn't she have family or friends who could help her? Didn't she have insurance? I posed all these questions to myself and then to her in a gentle manner. She apparently had no family, and the management where the fire had occurred had provided her with another duplex, but that was all. I also asked the question, which provided a response to the arrow prayer. "So what about insurance? Didn't you have any? Didn't your landlord require that of you?"

She looked down and then, in sad regret, back at me. "No, I didn't have any. They had told me it would be a good idea, but I really didn't want to pay the extra money for it. I thought I couldn't afford it. I never dreamed this would happen to me." She shook her head in remorse. "Little did I know that what I couldn't afford was to be without *anything*! I have nothing—no furniture, no clothes, none of the basic items most people just take for granted in their homes."

I listened to her despairing words in silent humility as she continued, "You just never think it could happen to you. I don't know how, when, or if I will ever recover," she said, her eyes brimming with tears.

She voluntarily continued to describe what had happened. "My next-door neighbor was smoking and fell asleep. I came home and found the fire department putting out the fire. I was in shock. Even now I can't believe it, but I have to go on. At least no one was hurt. My neighbor also lost everything and didn't have any insurance either. I know it's just things, but life is really hard without them."

I felt so badly for her and was finally able to express my sincere sympathy. I quickly bagged her items and walked around the counter. I hugged her and encouraged her to seek out services in the community that would help her.

She nodded and said, "It's hard to have to beg."

"No, it's not begging," I told her. "It's asking for help for an appropriate reason from those who can and want to give it."

I jotted down the names of local churches whose community outreach ministries would extend their hands to her. She thanked me and expressed gratitude that I had helped her. I wished her well and encouraged her to follow through on the information.

Well, you might be asking yourself if I was still in that complaining mood I mentioned earlier. No, no I wasn't. I had been enlightened and humbled within a matter of minutes. I wanted to go home and review that beautiful homeowner's policy I was paying for! I would never again complain about the price of protecting what I hold so dear—my home sweet home.

I Work with You: What's Your Name?

Have you ever had a misunderstanding with someone that caught you completely by surprise? You couldn't begin to understand, let alone explain, how it all started. It just did! And dealing with the confusion it created made for one of those memorable moments in life.

I had been transferred to a new department in order to promote a different product line, and I was looking forward to meeting the merchandiser assigned to the brand. Working in partnership with her would be key in generating more sales and, ultimately, achieving higher numbers for the brand. I wanted to familiarize myself with the core pieces and the way the product was displayed, so I decided to come in early one morning to introduce myself and offer my assistance.

I walked to my new area and didn't see anyone, so I checked the stockroom, and that's where I first met Laura, my merchandiser.

"Hi. My name is Pat, and I am the new specialist for the brand."

"Hello! I heard you were going to be working here. Welcome!"

We chatted for a few minutes and walked our sales floor. Laura displayed a passion and "eye" for her work, which made me eager to partner with her. We shared preliminary expectations, made small talk, and laughed congenially. The time went by quickly, and I needed to address the opening needs of my counter. As I prepared to go, I said, "I'm really looking forward to working with you, Laura. We're going to be a great team!"

"Yes, I agree. Thank you, Pat. I will see you later."

We were off to a great start!

In the months that followed, Laura and I enjoyed our working relationship, and our numbers reflected the goals we were striving for. Our friendship was also growing. We talked about our fashion ideas, families, hobbies, food, and the like.

One afternoon, I was informed of a large delivery due to arrive the following week. We had just received a big shipment, and I was concerned as to where we were going to put this anticipated merchandise. This was the type of situation in which I relied on Laura's expertise. I wrote myself a note to touch base with her in regard to the matter.

The next morning when I arrived at work, I went in search of Laura on the sales floor. I looked in all the obvious places but couldn't find her. I saw an area manager and asked if she had seen her. She responded that she didn't know who Laura was. *That's the craziest thing I've ever heard*, I thought to myself. *How can she not know who Laura is?*

I saw an assistant merchandiser and asked if she had seen Laura. "No, I haven't," she said. She paused and added, "Wait a minute. Who's Laura?"

Her response exasperated me. Perhaps, since she was somewhat new, she knew Laura by sight and not by name. Regardless, I needed to find Laura.

I spotted the lead merchandiser for the department adjacent to my brand. What a relief! I was absolutely certain she knew who Laura was and where I could find her. "Sandy! I'm so glad to see you!"

She greeted me warmly and stopped what she was doing as I approached her.

"Sandy, do you know where Laura is? It's the weirdest thing. No one seems to know who she is or where she is. I need to discuss that big shipment that's coming in with her!"

Sandy looked at me with a blank stare and said, "Pat, who's Laura? I don't know who that is."

I stood motionless for a moment and thought to myself, *What's happening? What's going on?* I felt a slight panic as my thoughts continued, *I know I've been working at this store for the last few months with a woman named Laura. Am I going crazy?*

I took a deep breath and said, "Sandy, are you pulling my leg? What's going on? Where's Laura?" I was quite serious, and she could tell I was concerned.

She calmly asked, "What does she look like, Pat?"

I responded in controlled alarm, "Sandy, are you kidding me? Really! Are you kidding me? I'm looking for Laura, the merchandiser for my brand. She's the cute, petite blonde—fair complexion, my height, sweet, hardworking! You know, *Laura!*"

Sandy was steady. I, however, seriously thought I was in the Twilight Zone! Sandy responded quietly and slowly, "Pat, the only person I know who has worked with you on your brand is Diana."

"Diana? Who is Diana?" I asked completely bewildered. "I don't know a Diana!"

She looked over my shoulder, pointed to the far corner, and said, "Over there; *that's* Diana."

I quickly turned to look, and there was Laura. I immediately responded, "No! *That's* Laura."

Sandy, maintained her composure and said, "No, Pat, her name is Diana! What made you think it was Laura?"

I was so stunned I could barely speak, but regardless, the words came out. "Well, for goodness' sake, I thought that was her name. That's what I've been calling her since I started the brand. She never said her name wasn't Laura! That's why I thought her name was Laura." Even though my explanation made no real sense, and we were equally perplexed, I thanked Sandy for her time and enlightenment.

I walked over to where Laura was prepping a display, and as I approached, she looked up and cheerfully greeted me, "Hi, Pat. Good morning!"

I gently took hold of her arm, looked her straight in the eye, and calmly asked, "What is your name?"

She shyly tilted her head and looked sheepishly at me. From that one look, I knew her name was ... *Diana!*

"Oh, Pat, you are so enthusiastic and sweet. I didn't have the heart to tell you my name wasn't Laura. You were always so happy to see me that, well, I decided I liked that name and you could call me Laura. I didn't have the heart to embarrass you."

For what felt like an *eternal* five seconds, I stood there mortified, and then it was as if a gentle breeze blew over me, and my heart overflowed with appreciation for my friend. Here for the last five months she had kindly accepted my calling her a name that wasn't her own. She hadn't wanted to hurt my feelings. I was so touched and said, "Your thoughtfulness toward me says everything about who you are. Thank you so much. But really, you *should* have told me!"

"No, I didn't want to. It was something special just between you and me," she responded.

"No! This was entirely just between you! I've been clueless," I said, jokingly scolding her.

I went on to tell her what had happened earlier that morning and how I had become annoyed at the new assistant merchandiser. I felt badly about that, but the more we talked about it, the funnier it was.

Sandy carefully approached and asked if everything was all right.

"Oh, Sandy, you must have thought I was crazy! Yes, everything is fine. I'd like to introduce you to, hmmm, is it Laura or Diana?"

The three of us engaged in the comedy of my error and after a time of shared laughter and conversation, we got straight to work.

Eight years have passed now. Initially, the story spread about the Diana/Laura mistaken-identity issue. Sure, it was a little embarrassing, but I comforted myself knowing I wasn't the only person ever to have called someone by the wrong name.

The truth is, to this very day, I still call Diana "Laura." It has become a term of endearment, and everyone knows that's my nickname for her. No one else calls her that or thinks I'm silly because I do. That's because "Laura" has graciously granted me that privilege, and it's something only special friends, like the two of us, can truly cherish!

The Impatient Shopper:
No Ifs, Ands, or Mothers

My goal is always to provide exceptional service, but delays in proceeding with a new transaction or assisting someone on the sales floor can happen for any number of reasons. I must confess, my favorite delay is when I'm able to take a brief moment to greet and have a word with one of my regular clients.

But delays, however brief, are not easy for some people to tolerate, as I was reminded of one morning.

My client, Elsie, and I had become friends through the years and had enjoyed numerous conversations, my favorites being those regarding travel. She and her husband were always off on an adventure to a destination far and away.

Elsie, who is absolutely charming, would often stop by my department and say hello, even when she was just passing through. Sometimes she would bring her gal pals and introduce them to me, and we would visit for a bit.

I was sorting some product in the adjacent department when Elsie approached in her typical delightful manner.

"Hello, my dear. There you are! I just wanted to say hello. What are you up to today?" she said.

I stood to give her a hug, and as I responded to her greeting, a woman interrupted us, not only with a harsh tone but also with assertive body language. You know what I mean—when someone crosses into your personal space and you're not sure if you should feel threatened or just chalk it up to bad manners.

"You! You work here, don't you? You can just finish this conversation with your mother some other time. Mother, you can call her later, or *you*," she added, pointing to me with the tilting of her head, "can call *her* later!"

The woman immediately proceeded to explain what she wanted, moving closer and closer as every word propelled from her mouth.

Elsie and I looked quizzically at one another and then at the woman.

Elsie tried to speak to her. "Ma'am, you are—"

But she was abruptly cut short. "Mother, please, finish this conversation later."

Elsie was shocked by the woman's words and behavior.

"Ma'am!" I interceded. "She is not my mother but, rather, my client, Elsie. And I will be right with you."

"Noooooo! I need you now! I need you *right now*!"

Elsie nervously said, "I'd best let you go, my dear. Will you be all right? Should I get someone to watch over you? Should I call someone?" Sweet Elsie was concerned about me.

"Elsie, don't you worry. I'll be just fine," I said, trying to calm and reassure her.

She clearly had been shaken by the woman's aggressiveness and walked slowly away, turning back to look at me as she left.

In the meantime, the intrusive woman didn't miss a beat with her demanding behavior. "Where are the flowered shirts? You should put them where people can see them! Where are they? I need one now."

I won't lie to you. I was so irritated that I wanted to do the bare minimum and just point her in the direction of the shirts, but I resisted the urge and escorted her to where they were located.

Her words continued to be negative and pressing. "Are these on sale? The flowers aren't very big! I wanted big flowers for the luau! I don't know if I like these colors! Do you even have my size? I don't know if I like this brand. Is it any good? Will I get a discount for buying one of these shirts?"

Just listening to her was causing my energy to spin like a whirlpool down a drain. She momentarily stopped to catch her breath, and I quickly jumped into her one-sided conversation. "They don't have much hanger appeal, ma'am, but they are some of our best sellers. And once you actually put them on, I'm sure you'll have a different opinion. Why don't we head over to one of our fitting rooms, and you can try on a few?"

My suggestion was instantly rejected. "Oh, no you don't! That's how you con people into buying a bunch of things they don't need. No way! I only want to try on one shirt because that's all I'm going to buy. I don't want to spend all day here."

I then made the mistake of asking which one she liked best, and that took her to an entirely new level of negativity. I suggested the pros and cons of different prints and colors, and she finally selected her one shirt to try on. I motioned with my hand for her to follow me to the fitting room.

As we walked, she continued to grumble and complain. "The parking lot was so crowded I had to park far away and then walk to get in here. Why are there are so many people in this store? Why is the air-conditioning on so cold? I'm warning you, those fitting room lines had better not be long and out the door, or else I'm going to walk out! I'd better get a discount on this shirt after going through all this trouble."

It was impossible for me to respond to anything she said because she didn't speak with the intention of receiving an answer but rather of making her own opinions and feelings known. I could only nod my head as I directed her to an open fitting room.

Three minutes at most passed, and she emerged. With a wave of the lucky luau shirt in her hand, she said, "I guess this will have to do. Ring it up, will you? I'm in a hurry. No talking. Just ring it up!" I did as I was told and said nothing.

In her gruff manner, she continued, "I hope you and your mother can talk later. You tell her I said thank you and that you were a big help to me today." Since she had finally said something positive, I didn't attempt to correct the misperception she had so indelibly established in her mind about my "mother."

"I will be sure to let her know, ma'am."

As I began to walk around the counter to hand her the bag, she stopped me midway and snatched it from my hand. She began to rant about all the other things she had to do that day. It was quite sad, as she seemed so miserable; yet some people are in their "happy place" when they're complaining.

On Elsie's next visit to the store, she sought me out and said, "Oh dear, I hated leaving you with that awful woman. Were you all right?"

I responded, "Yes, Mother, I was! Thank you for being so understanding in that situation. She actually wanted me to thank you and tell you that I had been a big help to her."

It took Elsie a moment and then the oddity of the circumstance struck her. We both laughed out loud as we understood our new "mother/ daughter" relationship to be the bright side of the situation. Only then could we say we were appreciative of the woman's interruption.

Interesting, isn't it, how precious bonds are developed with those who touch our lives? At least that's what "Mama Elsie" and I think!

Return Transactions, All with a Reason

Customers return items to my counter approximately fifty times on a typical sales day. Most returns are routine and processed quickly. However, there are those with a story, which provide a window, and I'm given the opportunity to look through and see human nature revealed in a unique way. Prepare yourself, as you, too, look inside and discover the personalities, emotions, and intentions behind return transactions.

The woman threw her bag on the counter and said in an agitated tone, "I don't know if I can return this. It's been over five months! And do you want to know *why* it's been over five months?" she asked intently.

I relaxed my stance and leaned slightly into the counter, curious as to what she was going to say.

"Because I asked my husband to return it. *That's why*!"

Although I remained silent, I couldn't help but raise my eyebrows.

The woman appeared to be in control for a moment, but as she recalled the incident, she got worked up, and her voice intensified. "He even had the nerve to tell me he had returned it!"

She shook her head and let out a disgusted sigh. She grabbed the bag off the counter and shook it, as she continued, "Last night I needed a flashlight. I knew he had one in the backseat compartment of his truck, so I went to get it. That's when I saw the store bag sticking out from underneath the seat!" She threw the bag down on the counter in frustration. "He came running out to the truck, saw that I had found the bag, and started up with his excuses. I'm so mad at that man! I just should have returned the sweater myself."

I calmly asked if I could take the sweater and return it for her.

"*What*! Do you mean to tell me you can take it back after all this time? Are you going to get in trouble? I don't want to get you fired!"

I smiled and said, "Absolutely not, ma'am." As the words came out of my mouth, the return was processing, and I directed her to sign on the signature pad.

"There! It's all done. No worries!"

"*Really*! That's it? That was all I had to do?"

I laughed and said, "Yes, ma'am. That's it!"

She sighed in relief and thanked me.

"Now then," I said, "may I recommend some adorable tops we just got in?" I winked, suggesting she do some shopping.

She got my cue and said, "Girl, you bet I'm going to shop, and I'm going to shop *good!* Will you ring me up when I'm ready?"

"I'll be happy to!"

We laughed as her frustration lifted, and she turned to face the beautiful clothing before her.

Yes, she was definitely ready to shop!

I greeted the young woman as she took her turn at my counter and asked, "May I return some pajamas here?"

"Yes, of course!"

She proceeded to explain why she was returning the pajamas. "Every single year," she began, slowly enunciating each word in frustration, "without fail, Mother buys my husband and me pajamas for Christmas. I've tried to tell her nicely that we don't need them, but she won't listen. Truth is, my husband and I sleep naked, but I don't feel comfortable telling my mother that. I'm sure you know what I mean. Daddy must have worn pajamas and she certainly does, so she just assumes that we wear them too. Look at these!"

She held up a pair of flannel pajamas that were so loud they could keep a bear from hibernating. I let out a slight gasp and was unable to control my horrified facial expression. I nodded my head in understanding of her predicament.

"My husband insisted I return them because they are so hideous! I just don't know what she was thinking!"

I took the pajamas and said, "You needn't say another word. I get it! Let me return them for you."

Her refund amount was slightly over sixty dollars. I handed her a gift card, and she responded, "I'm off to the shoe department to buy some gorgeous heels. Now *those* my husband loves."

We laughed as she left my counter, joyful to be rid of the Christmas pajamas—until next year, that is!

I hung them up and immediately placed them on a rack to be sent back to their proper department. I also made a mental note never to purchase pajamas for my grown children unless they asked!

A group of four women and two men approached my counter thirty minutes prior to our closing on a Sunday night. The timing of this return had been carefully planned, and I would soon learn why.

One of the women, who appeared to be in her early thirties, placed numerous bags on the counter and quietly said, "I need to return all of this. It was bought at separate times, and it's a variety of things. Please, may I just do it all here?"

"Of course! I'll take care of it for you right now."

Her hands trembled as she slowly emptied each bag of its contents, taking long glances at specific pieces and finally just flipping all the bags over. She shook her head as she gently picked up one dress in particular, held it to her chest and laid it back down. She appeared to be in shock, numb, as she said to no one in particular, "I just can't believe this is happening. I just can't!"

She turned to step away from the counter and as she did, her tears began to flow as though the floodgates of her heart had been yanked opened. Two of the women accompanying her stepped away with her.

It was distressing to watch her cry so deeply. I tried not to stare and stayed focused on the transaction. I relayed each amount to those in her party who had remained at the counter. One of them, her sister, proceeded to tell me what the return was all about.

"Katy was going to be married in two weeks. She and Thomas had been together for twelve years. A series of excruciating events revealed Thomas's true nature, and Katy immediately had to call off the wedding. To say the least, her world has been turned upside down, and we're trying to help her close all the details pertaining to the wedding. We hated coming in just as you were about to close, but we didn't want to do this during the day when the store is so busy and crowded. It's difficult enough for her as it is!"

I assured her it was no trouble at all and that she shouldn't worry; I would be finished shortly. It was evident the betrayal had impacted the entire family, and I felt badly for all of them. Katy continued to cry and voice heartfelt questions, which we all could hear but no one could answer.

One of the men at the counter said, "Cowardly excuse for a man. I'm looking forward to seeing him face-to-face one day. I want him to explain his actions to me before I beat the daylights out of him."

I looked at him with understanding, knowing he was trying to cope with Katy's sobs.

I completed the transaction. On my counter were lovely dresses, bathing suits, lingerie, shorts, pants, tops and handbags—everything returned with a crushed heart. I handed the receipt to the sister who had opened the conversational window, and I walked around the counter to approach Katy. I gently placed my hand on her shoulder, and she looked at me with swollen, tear-soaked eyes that expressed wrenching pain.

I spoke encouragingly to her. "I'm so proud of you, honey. What you just did took so much courage. You're going to come out of this, and in time, you will love again."

She mouthed a "thank you" and nodded her head.

I commended the entire group for standing together and they responded with appreciation. They were a family with an incredible bond of love and strength, and I held them in high regard as they walked away.

I returned to my counter, which was covered with lovely items, selected with thoughtfulness and romance in mind, and I couldn't help but hope that Katy's brother got his wish!

A lovely young woman, in what appeared to be her late teens to early twenties, approached my counter and said she would like to return a shirt.

Nothing unusual about that, I thought to myself, assuring her I could assist her.

"I bought this for my mom, hoping she would get well and be able to wear it, but she never did. She died."

Her words, spoken somewhat casually, stunned me.

"I showed it to her, and she liked it. But she never wore it, never even tried it on. She was fine one day and the next day got super sick and died. I still can't believe my mom's gone!" She sighed deeply and stared at me in disbelief.

I walked around the counter and stood by her side. "Oh, sweetheart, I'm so sorry. Are you here by yourself?"

She responded that she was and continued, "She died a month ago, but I just didn't want to return the shirt. I wanted to keep it because it was the last thing I ever bought her that she got to see. Keeping it reminds me of how sick she was. It makes me sad, but at the same time, it makes me feel connected to her. I feel confused and don't know what to do. Should I return it or keep it?"

This was by no means a typical return!

I was deeply touched by this sweet girl and thought to myself, *If she were my daughter what would I want someone to say to her?*

"Honey, I can't answer that for you, but what I can confidently tell you is that your mama would want you to remember her happy and healthy. She wouldn't want you to agonize like this. This shirt, this piece of clothing, should not be causing you such pain and heartache. You and your mama spent years together, and this shirt represents just a small bit of time, a painful time. Hold on to the good memories and what brings you comfort. The truth is, you bought this with an expectation that didn't turn out the way you'd hoped. That's not anyone's fault, sweetheart. But if you were my girl, I would want you to let it go and recall all that was good and loving. Don't you think that's what your mama would want as well?"

I could tell she was pondering the question. It took a moment, but a smile came forth as she nodded with a glimmer of hope and comfort, saying, "Yes, I know my mom would want that. Wow, just hearing you say those things has made me feel better. I don't feel so confused anymore. So can I return the shirt to you?"

I smiled and walked back to my side of the counter. "Yes, you can. Are you ready?" I asked.

"Yes, I am. I'd like to return this shirt!" she said confidently.

I processed the return and handed her the receipt. She stood there for a moment, touched the shirt, and looked at me with tears in her eyes. "Thank you for helping me," she said with childlike sincerity.

Once again, I walked around the counter and gave her a hug. I looked deep into her eyes and saw that death had challenged the innocence of her young life. I told her that her life would reflect her mama, and that she would make her proud. She nodded and smiled sweetly.

As she turned and walked away, I looked at the shirt she had lovingly bought for her mama lying on my counter and couldn't help but feel an ache in my heart.

A few days after Christmas, two women approached my counter with a box containing a cable-knit sweater.

"I'd like to return this, please. It's much too big for me," said the younger woman of the two.

I nodded and proceeded to process her return. As I did, both women talked about the sweater and wondered how the young woman's mother-in-law could have thought she wore an extra large. Just from glancing at her it was obvious she was a definite size small.

I immediately got the feeling it was one of "those" Christmas gifts— you know, the type given with little or no regard and meant to hurt the recipient's feelings. As the return processed, my intuition was validated. I looked at my screen and saw that her mother-in-law had paid $6.15 for her Christmas gift.

I braced myself as I gave her the information. "Ma'am, the return amount is for $6.15."

"What! What did you say? *Six dollars and fifteen cents*? Are you sure? Is that what she paid for it or is that the amount that's being given back because it's after Christmas?" she asked, hoping there was some mistake.

"No, I'm so sorry. That's what she paid for it," I softly responded.

Turning to her mother, the young woman erupted. "Mother, do you see what I mean? She absolutely hates me! She spent $6.15 on me for *Christmas*! I've done nothing to make her treat me like this. I'm a good

wife and mother, but she just hates me. Now you actually get to see what I constantly have to deal with!"

The mother could not believe it. She calmly picked up the sweater and asked me how the return amounts were processed. I explained, but my answer brought no excuse or comfort for the mother-in-law's behavior.

The mother spoke to me in a very soft, controlled manner. "You know, I have always treated Craig, my son-in-law, as though he were my own son. I give him the best I can. His mother, on the other hand, is filthy rich. She does this purposely to hurt my daughter, not only with the price but with the size as well."

I felt badly for the mother because she was trying to remain composed, yet the obvious rejection of her daughter by her mother-in-law was quite disturbing to her.

The daughter began to cry. "I just don't know what to do anymore. This is so embarrassing."

I understood all too well and said, "Honey, this says absolutely nothing about you but everything about her. Believe me, I understand how much it hurts, and you needn't feel embarrassed."

"You are so right," the mother said as her daughter wiped her eyes. "Nonetheless, it's shocking to see it so blatantly acted out, especially at Christmas."

I nodded in agreement and deeply sympathized with both of them. I waited a few moments and then gently asked what she would like to do with the sweater.

"I don't know! What should I do, Mother?"

Her mother was at a loss as well.

After some thought, the young woman decided, "I'm going to take it back home. I want to show my husband and see what he thinks we should do."

I placed the box containing the sweater in a bag and wished her the best. They thanked me and said good-bye.

I thought of that young woman many times in the days that followed. I sincerely hoped she and her husband would find a way to deal with her mother-in-law's behavior before it created irreparable damage.

A couple who appeared to be in their late fifties was returning the Christmas gifts their son had purchased for them. They said the gifts were not to their liking.

The mother's gift, a handbag, had a return amount of $42.50, and the father's gift, a shirt, was $24.99, for a total return amount, with tax, of $72.55. Upon hearing this, the couple looked at one another in disbelief and seemed extremely offended. The father asked if I was certain of the refund amounts.

"Yes, I am," I replied and explained the return procedure to them.

They stood looking at the gifts, dissecting their overall appearance, and discussing the cost of each one in detail. They asked about the brands and whether or not they had been on sale when their son had bought them. They asked how he'd paid for them and when he'd bought them. I responded to each question but felt very uncomfortable doing so. I was especially hesitant to tell them that he had purchased the gifts on December 24, Christmas Eve. Sure enough, the mother responded that he had more than likely waited until the last minute in order to get the cheapest price.

My curiosity got the better of me, and I asked how old the son was. "Oh, he's twenty, a college student, but that doesn't excuse these cheap gifts."

I decided to go to bat for the son. "Folks, the truth is, these items aren't 'cheap' in terms of the quality and brand. Originally, the handbag was eighty-five dollars, and the shirt was fifty dollars. Both items were 50 percent off at the time he purchased them. The fact that an item is on sale doesn't affect the quality. It's simply that we reduce the price to move the merchandise through its shelf life."

They would have absolutely none of what I was saying! The father turned to the mother and said, "If he thinks he's going to get away with this, he's got another thing coming. This is a joke. We're his parents, and this is what he spends on us!" The mother looked at the gifts and shook her head in displeasure.

I suggested that perhaps they might find something in the store to their liking and do an exchange. However, once again, my suggestion was rebuffed. The father gruffly instructed me to complete the return transaction. I proceeded as directed and handed them the cash that was due them for the return.

"Why, that won't even buy us a decent dinner," the mother complained.

The father was even more chilling, as he turned to me and said, "Well, well, well! He's going to have to learn a lesson. He'll just have to wait and see what he gets for this, won't he?"

I tried to lighten the moment by saying that they weren't walking away completely empty-handed. They did have some cash in hand! They smirked at me and walked away bitter and disgruntled.

Their responses and behavior were unsettling, and I couldn't help but feel anxious for their son. I wondered what exactly they wanted from him and what he could have purchased that would have made them happy. What dollar amount did he need to spend in order to satisfy them?

I reflected on the gifts my children had given me at Christmas when they were young. It was a ritual. Every year when they asked what I wanted, I'd respond that I wanted them to write me a letter. Yes, those Christmas letters, handwritten with drawings and sentiments from my children's hearts, were my gifts from them—priceless treasures that this couple never would have understood or appreciated.

A woman excitedly approached me holding a black tweed jacket, interwoven with gold, shimmering thread. It had large, gaudy, black-and-gold buttons.

"Could you try this on for me? My granddaughter is about your size, and I think this will fit her."

"I run between a small and medium, ma'am. Is that her size also?"

"Well, no! This jacket is an extra large, but you're quite busty, so I think it will fit you," she responded confidently.

I sighed and thought, *Really?*

I put the jacket on, and it was, without a doubt, too big for me.

The woman failed to see it that way and exclaimed, "Oh, it's perfect!"

"What? No, ma'am, it's not! I can tell by the feel of the jacket. Here, let's walk over to the mirror, and I will show you how it's hanging on my body."

She begrudgingly followed me to the mirror, and I showed her where the jacket fell on my shoulders, waist, and yes, my busty chest. Overall, it was just too large! Despite the visual, she wouldn't budge. I took the jacket off and handed it back to her.

"Ma'am, perhaps I can order you one in her proper size. Let me look it up for you." She continued to insist that, in her opinion, it looked fine. But I respectfully disagreed and told her so.

Unfortunately, there were no similar jackets remaining in the system. She was holding the last one.

"Well, that's fine because I think it's going to fit her beautifully, so I'm going to get it!"

I rang the transaction, and she was delighted to hear that the jacket had been reduced from its original price of nearly a hundred dollars down to less than twenty-five dollars.

"I hope your granddaughter enjoys the jacket," I said.

She assured me in a condescending tone that not only would she *love* the jacket but it would *fit* her as well.

I smiled as I handed her the bag and wished her a nice day.

Approximately two weeks later, a woman approached my counter and said, "I need to return a gift.

"Check this out!" she said, pulling out the black tweed jacket with the gold shimmer threading and gaudy buttons.

My eyes widened as I grabbed the jacket and looked at the woman in complete surprise! "You are not going to believe this, but I sold this jacket to the lady who gave it to you! She insisted it fit me and that it would definitely fit you! Believe me, I tried to—"

The woman interrupted me midsentence. "You don't have to explain. That woman is my grandmother. She is so controlling that, if you disagree with her, she will unmercifully pressure you until you buckle. But when I saw this thing," she smacked the jacket with the back of her hand, "there was *no way* I was going to keep it, wear it, or do anything but return it! When I showed her that it didn't fit, she told me I was seeing things! Can you believe that?"

I nodded my head in complete understanding, as I clearly recalled the grandmother's behavior when I had tried the jacket on.

"My cousin even told her it didn't fit me, and she still refused to accept the reality of this ugly thing. After a few minutes of going back and forth about the fit, she seemed to weaken a little, which is no small thing for my grandmother. She called her alterations lady to ask if we could come over and have her fix it. I had to raise my voice to her and downright refuse the jacket. She acted dejected and abused and made me feel guilty. I tried to explain that it just wasn't my taste in clothing, and the size was definitely off. She got mad and told me in her bossy, know-it-all way that I knew nothing about style and that this jacket would have added so much to my wardrobe."

The woman was emotionally and physically exhausting herself explaining the scenario. I interjected, explaining briefly what had happened when her grandmother was in the store.

She gasped when I mentioned my "busty chest" and covered her face with her hands. "Oh my God, I'm so sorry!"

I laughed and told her she needn't be sorry, as I had dealt with her grandmother's type many times before.

The young woman continued to vent about the jacket and her grandmother. It was evident she needed to rid herself of the frustration that the gift had caused. In the end, the grandmother had said to take the jacket and do whatever she wanted with it but that she would always remember this act of ungratefulness and would never buy her anything again.

Interestingly, at this point in her narration, a huge smile lit up the young woman's face. "So, I'm returning it, and am going to buy something else!" she said triumphantly.

In my world, the jacket had come full circle, from its purchase to its return. I handed her a gift card, and although it wasn't much, she was very happy. It was as if her joy came not from the refund amount but rather from having taken a stand against her grandmother and having won.

Truth is after having met the woman myself, I couldn't have been happier for her.

The return had been the gift within the gift!

So there you have it—a peek inside the window of return transactions. Next time you must wait in line while someone is explaining his or her reasons for a return, I hope you will be understanding and patient. Just remember, on another day, that could be *your* return window wide open at the counter!

Retail Therapy: The Free Hug

People shop for numerous reasons, some because they actually need the clothes they're buying, others for the sake of escaping their reality by means of "retail therapy." Such was the case of a young woman who approached my counter.

I had noticed three women who had been shopping for quite some time. Although my partners and I had reached out to assist them, they preferred to shop on their own. When they came out of the fitting rooms, they proceeded to get in line to wait their turn. One of my partners was going to lunch and asked me to take over at the back register, where I called the next customer. It was one of the women who had been shopping all afternoon.

"Hi. How are you? Here, let me take those things from you."

The young woman thanked me as I began the process of sorting the many items she was intending to purchase

"I'm sorry there are so many clothes. I just kind of went crazy. Can you tell me the prices as you ring them up, and I will make my decision on each one as we go?"

"Of course, not a problem. Let me get everything ready and don't hesitate to tell me what you want to do!"

I heard her sigh deeply. Most customers show some enthusiasm when they're buying this much product but not this woman. She stood solemnly, occasionally picking up an item and then tossing it back in the pile. I could hear her girlfriends at the counter behind me asking questions and excitedly discussing which selection they were planning on wearing that night.

As I quoted the price of each item, she was in agreement with everything, but at one point, she stopped and said, "I just don't know if I even need any of these things. It's eighty degrees outside. Do I really want this leather jacket?" She was sincerely asking me to respond to her question.

I put my scanner down and looked directly at her. "Miss, why are you buying all these clothes? You don't really seem to be enthusiastic about your purchases. What's going on?" I asked gently.

She looked at me, and her eyes welled with tears. "Today is the anniversary of my twin brother's death. I'm standing here, and yet I'm not. My heart is broken, and I'm just shopping to shop. My friends insisted that I come with them to distract myself from the pain, but the truth is that my heart will never be distracted from losing him."

As we looked intently at one another, I reached over the counter and took her hand. "Sweetheart, it's okay. You don't have to buy any of this if you don't want to. But if you do, then that's okay too! I'm sure your brother wouldn't want your heart to be weighed down like this." With the pile of clothes still on the counter I asked, "Which one of these pieces do you think he would have liked? Maybe you could buy the one that would have been his favorite."

My question triggered something within her, and a soft smile arose as she picked a few pieces. Then she said, "It's okay, I'm going to get them all. Can I bring them back if I decide I don't want them?"

"Yes, absolutely!" I responded.

"Okay! Then I want them all!"

As I continued with the transaction, she began to open up, "I don't know what to do. My friends want me to go out with them tonight, but I don't know if I should. I don't feel strong enough. I just want to be alone. What should I do?" Once again she proposed her question with such sincerity that it prompted me to share my opinion.

"Sounds to me like you have friends who love and care about you as though they were your family! They don't want you to be alone."

She looked at me, and more tears filled her eyes. She forced a smile and said, "You're right. Thank you for being so honest."

"Going out doesn't dismiss the pain or betray your brother's memory. Bottom line, do what makes you feel better. Ironically, sometimes that means doing the opposite of what we think we want. Do you understand what I'm saying?"

At that moment, her friends approached and asked what she was buying.

"I'm getting it all," she responded.

"*All* of it?" they exclaimed and laughed.

"Yes, all of it."

"What are you wearing tonight?" one of them asked.

She shrugged her shoulders and said, "I'm still not sure I'm even going."

Her friends lovingly urged her to join them that evening and then stepped away to the ladies' room while I finished her transaction. When I was done wrapping and bagging her items, I walked around the counter, and we met face-to-face.

"Honey, may I give you a hug?"

This precious young woman stood before me with tears falling from her eyes. She gently nodded her head because her quivering lips wouldn't let the "yes" come out of her mouth. At that moment it was as though she were my daughter, and I hugged her deeply. She briefly cried on my shoulder and then stepped back, wiped her eyes, and thanked me for listening to her and ringing up her transaction.

"It was my pleasure. Take care of yourself, okay?"

As she walked away I extended peace and comfort toward her and hoped she would take advantage of her friends' invitation.

Weeks passed and once again I was working at the back register. I called the next person in line, a young woman. As with every customer, I welcomed her and struck up a conversation about her selections.

She responded to my questions and then asked, "Do you remember me?"

She indeed looked familiar, but I couldn't place the circumstance under which I had helped her and gently told her so, with an apology.

"Oh, it's okay. I came shopping on the anniversary of my brother's death. You were so nice to me. You hugged and comforted me. Your touch did something to me. I can't explain it, but it did. People have no idea how powerful a hug can be, and yours meant the world to me that day."

I looked closely at her, and yes, of course, I recalled who she was. I reached over the counter and took her hand. "It's so great to see you. How are you? Tell me, did you go out that night with your friends?"

She seemed surprised I had remembered about the invitation and said, "Yes, I did. It was hard, but I did it!"

We continued to chat, and she once again expressed appreciation for my words of comfort and especially for the hug.

"I was feeling so badly that day and when you hugged me, well, it just helped. You were a stranger, and yet you still hugged me."

I told her I was glad to have been able to offer some solace.

She placed a large bag on the counter, "You said it would be okay to return anything if I didn't want it, right?"

We both laughed.

"I absolutely did say that! My word is good!"

I processed the return as well as some new items she had selected. When I was done, I walked around the counter and said, "Now this time I want to give you a happy hug."

She laughed, and her lovely face lit up with a smile that would have made her twin brother proud.

It was "retail therapy" at its best!

Spoken Perfectly, My Birth Name

I was going through a very difficult time in my life, and I was deeply discouraged. My faith was the only thing I clung to as I tried to persevere. However, every day I prayed for the opportunity of being His hand extended—a comforter to someone who needed help or an uplifting word. I also asked that I would find encouragement and hope for better days in my future. Little did I know that, on one day, my prayer would be answered in a most unusual manner.

It was a busy Saturday morning, and every coworker in my department was working. The lines to purchase were long, and the fitting rooms were occupied with women taking advantage of the store's sales prices. I was busy out on the sales floor, answering questions about products and directing customers to the specific departments they were looking for.

A young woman who was new to our department asked if I would assist a customer she didn't feel she could adequately help. She directed me to the area where the elderly couple was sitting, and I introduced myself.

The husband responded to my greeting and said, "This is my wife, Gloria. She had a stroke a year ago and has difficulty talking and expressing herself. She needs your help in the changing room with trying on clothes. Will you help her? I'm going to sit right here, and you can get her whatever she needs."

"I'd be happy to help. Hello, Gloria. My name is Pat. I will be assisting you today. Do you have something specific you're wanting to shop for?"

She grabbed my arm, and by squeezing it and pointing with her cane, she began to direct me. "Shirts. Bright shirts. Small," she said in a slow, staggered manner. "That," she struggled to say as she pointed to a woman wearing a polo shirt.

"You want some polo shirts?" I asked.

She nodded.

"Is there anything else you would like to shop for today?"

She shook her head, "No."

"Gloria, we have a variety of polo shirts by different designers. Would you prefer to wait here with your husband while I select an assortment, and then you can try them on?"

"No, I ... go."

Her husband reassured me, "Oh, she's okay. She'll let you know if she gets tired. I'll be right here. You can take all the time you need."

I advised my partners I would be out of the department and unavailable for a while, and with that done, Gloria and I began our shopping.

Gloria really seemed to enjoy selecting the bright-colored polo shirts that we offered. I collected them, and she let me know she wanted to continue browsing. We would stop and look at clothing that would catch her eye, and I would describe the different types of looks she could achieve with each one. In reality, I knew she was still recovering, and only basics were feasible for her present lifestyle.

Although it was difficult for her, she made the effort to speak to me. She would become confused and easily agitated when she couldn't get the words out that she wanted.

I felt badly for her, and yet I admired her. She was a determined woman, and her willingness to take my arm and guide me with her actions demonstrated her fiery spirit.

After thirty minutes or so, she said she was tired. I asked if she wanted to try the shirts on.

She said yes by nodding her head.

We walked slowly toward the fitting rooms and found one with a long bench for her to sit on. I laid the shirts next to her and asked if she was ready for me to help her change.

"Yes," she nodded once again.

As I bent down to pull her shirt over her head, she touched my head of curls and shook her head with a tender smile. It was her way of telling me she liked them.

"Pretty ... not me." She shook her head and added, "No ... more."

I thanked her for her kind words and said, "Gloria, you've been through a lot, but that doesn't mean you're not pretty. Why just look! Do you see how lovely you look in this coral polo?"

She turned slowly toward the mirror and smiled a crooked smile of approval.

She tried on each piece, and when we were done, she had selected five shirts in various colors.

I put her original shirt back on and straightened her collar and buttons. I did my best to fix her hair so it didn't appear as though she'd been trying on clothes. She looked in the mirror, appreciating my efforts, and thanked me.

"It's my pleasure, dear," I responded sincerely.

As I brought her cane close to her, I explained that I wanted her to get up slowly. At that moment, I looked down and noticed her tennis shoe had come untied. I bent down on one knee and then thought it best to retie both shoes for safety's sake.

As I went to stand, Gloria's hands stopped me at my shoulders. She held them there and with absolute ease, clarity and concentration, looked me in the eye and said, "Patricia Elizabeth, God is going to bless you!"

She stared intently at me and then quickly reverted, dropped her hands to her lap, and began to fiddle with her cane.

I was stunned! I looked at my name tag. "Pat," it said simply. Again I looked at her, and then I looked above to the ceiling. Gloria had called me by my *birth name*, Patricia Elizabeth! We hadn't discussed names, much less birth names! Furthermore, I generally go by Pat. Rarely does someone call me Patricia. I knew instantly my prayer for encouragement and hope for better days had been answered. Gloria seemed in no way affected by her words, almost as though she had never spoken them, but in fact she had!

I helped her up and led her to the reception area to sit down while I went to get her husband. Upon their reunion, he admired the shirts

she had selected and paid for them. He thanked me for helping her and hoped it hadn't been too much trouble for me.

"No trouble at all, sir." I placed my hand on Gloria's arm and said, "Good-bye, Gloria. Thank you so much."

She shook her cane and sweetly smiled her crooked smile. They turned and walked slowly out of the department. I returned to my department to let my partners know I had finished with my customer and was going to lunch.

As I ate, I reflected on my experience with Gloria. I thought about the clarity and focus of her words in that moment compared to her speech during the previous hour we had been together. I tried to estimate the likelihood of her guessing my middle name and marveled at how she had spoken my full birth name. I carefully pondered her words "God *is going to* bless you," rather than "God bless you." Finally, I thought about how the circumstance had occurred. I was on my knees, helping her, which is my daily prayer. I had been called by my birth name and given hope that blessings were indeed in my future. How remarkable and unexplainable! But then again, that's what faith is all about. I felt hope rise up within me. I felt comforted.

I would see Gloria and her husband in the store on two other occasions, but she didn't remember me. Considering her health, I understood. But I remembered Gloria! The truth is, I will remember her all the days of my life. The customer who was referred to me by another associate because she didn't feel capable was actually destined to be mine that day.

In assisting Gloria, I was inspired that each person in this world has value and something to offer, despite our human assumptions. We are *all* meant to fulfill a purpose as each day unfolds and that is exactly what Gloria and I had done for one another.

Amazing, isn't it, the things that can be accomplished in one hour of shopping!

The Dream Come True:
The Night I Worked My Wand

Walt Disney's Cinderella *has always been one of my favorite animated movies. There are so many things about it that are endearing to my heart.*

As the store geared down from its weekend sale, I had an experience that would remind me of Cinderella and give me even more appreciation for the role of her fairy godmother. Granted, this time there would be no pumpkins, horses, dogs, or mice—only delightful wonders performed with a modern twist!

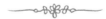

Sundays are my Fridays. I was finishing up with my last customer, and then I would be off, ready to start my "weekend." Melissa and I had enjoyed working together and I had even opened an account for her. She had purchased numerous items, and I wanted to put them in a shopping bag rather than the plastic bags that were ready at my counter.

"Melissa, please let me go across the way to the personal shopper's office and get a bag for you."

"That would be great. I would really appreciate that very much," she responded.

As I approached the office, I saw Mitchell, our men's personal shopper, standing outside talking with a Latino family of five.

I walked by, and he called out to me, "Pat, could you help me out here? These nice folks are looking for some pants and a few other items for their mom. Could you assist them with that?"

I'll be honest, my initial thought was, *I'm not going to be starting my weekend as soon as I had hoped.* However, my respect for Mitchell was such that there was no way I would deny his request.

"Of course, Mitchell. Just let me get a few shopping bags and finish up with the customer at my counter, and then I'll be ready to help."

The son turned to his mother and spoke to her in Spanish, explaining the situation. I greeted them in Spanish and invited them to join me in my department, where I would be happy to assist them. The family kindly returned my greeting and agreed to follow me.

Mitchell was appreciative that I was taking over and quite surprised I could speak fluent Spanish. "I didn't know that about you," he said.

I teased and said, "It's all about timing. I knew you needed my help. The bags were just an excuse to come over here."

We both laughed as I turned to go.

As the family followed, I tried not to appear rude as I walked briskly back to my counter, where Melissa was patiently waiting.

When she saw me and the family following right behind, she laughed and said, "Well, I'm not surprised you picked up customers along the way."

I thanked her for being so understanding and carefully bagged her items. I wished her a great evening and she was set to go, happy with her purchases.

I turned my attention to the family and learned they were on a shopping trip from the Lake Tahoe area. The family consisted of a mother, son, nephew, and two daughters. The store was due to close in just a few hours, and the young adults wanted to get some shopping of their own done prior to heading home.

"Pati, I would like for you to help my mother find whatever she needs," said the son. "She has been through so much this past year. I want this to be a special time for her to find things that will make her look and feel good. Cost is no problem. Please, just do your best for our mother."

I was so touched by this young man's heart toward his mother. He wanted her taken care of, and I assured him I would do just that. They all said good-bye, and I was left alone with his mother, Consuelo.

I sensed that Consuelo needed to be put at ease, and I shared that I was from El Salvador. She in turn said she was from Panama. I spoke gently to her in Spanish and said we would have fun finding her some lovely clothes. I asked if she knew her size and if there was anything in particular she really wanted to buy. Consuelo was in awe of all of the clothing in my department.

"It's all so beautiful, just beautiful! But Pati, before we start, I need to tell you something," she said. "I was in a very bad car accident and severely injured my leg. I'm fortunate I didn't lose it, but now I walk with a slight limp. In addition, I have to wear a brace to strengthen and support my leg. I haven't been able to do much, and I've put on a lot of weight. I have been wearing these same pants now for many weeks, and I've been very depressed. My son thought a trip out of our home town and a visit to this lovely mall would cheer us up, and I could find some clothes." Her brown eyes released tears as she sighed in deep despair.

"Consuelo, I am going to help you. Please don't worry about the brace. I made a promise to your son that I would take care of you, and now I make that promise to you. Let's enjoy our time shopping!"

Due to her injury, I didn't want her to strain by walking more than she needed to. She would have to conserve her energies for trying on clothes in the fitting room. I encouraged her to browse in the areas closest to the reception area, in case she needed to sit down and rest. In the meantime, I went about and selected numerous pieces for her to try on. Consuelo was only about five feet tall and wore a size 10. I was trying to be thoughtful as to her weight concern and help her find things she could wear with her brace.

After a bit, with various items in hand, I asked if she would like my help in the fitting room. She laughed and said, "Yes, you'd better help me. Some of these clothes look unlike anything I have ever worn before. I won't know what to do with them." Consuelo appeared almost innocent in her excitement.

I arranged the outfits for her to try on while she undressed. I asked if there was one in particular she wanted to try on first.

"Any one is fine. They are all beautiful. Ayyy, I'm so nervous," she said.

I laughed and told her the best was yet to come. Consuelo then did something I had never seen before. She closed the mirrored panels before she put the clothing on. I discerned her injury had damaged not only her leg but also her self-esteem. She didn't want to look at herself in the brace. We slipped on some black Capri pants that had faux diamond stud buttons and were cinched at the ankle, providing an adjustable length. I teamed the Capris with a yellow-and-black top. The color combination was lovely with her skin tone, as the yellow was the perfect hue. I got her completely settled in the outfit and tidied her hair.

"Consuelo, do you want to look in the mirror?"

She was visibly nervous and let out a sigh, "Yes, I want to see myself."

She once again did something I had never seen before. She closed her eyes. I laughed with excitement and opened the mirrored panels.

"Look, Consuelo! Open your eyes. You're so lovely!"

She stood motionless, her eyes roving up and down. She breathed deeply and began to cry. "I look like I am normal, like there is nothing wrong with me."

"You look beautiful!" I said as I stood beside her. "Look at the back of the shirt. See how nice it looks on you."

I adjusted the mirrors so she could see from behind. She liked what she saw and was cautiously ready for more.

Her anxiety was slowly calming and she began to share about the heartaches she had endured in the last year. This moment in time was something she had dreamed of when she was bedridden, and now her dream was coming true.

She told me she had been afraid to come into the store. She thought she would be looked down upon for being a Latina and not very well dressed. She shared honestly that, at first, she'd felt a little unsure about working with me. I stopped what I was doing and gave her a hug. I looked into her eyes and said that I was honored to be the one to help her and that she needn't worry about anything. There was such a sweet, humble spirit about her, which made me want to make everything perfect for her.

"Consuelo, are you ready for another outfit? Now we're going to try this one." I held up a pair of dark brown Capris and a multitoned, brown, chiffon top with cold-shoulder sleeves.

Again, she closed the mirrors and her eyes before she would take a look at herself. I carefully adjusted everything about the outfit and made sure she was all set.

"May I open the mirrors for you?"

"Yes, okay! I'm ready," she said.

Her first expression was one of sheer surprise and then her face lit up. She smiled as she, like Cinderella, touched the clothing and turned from side to side. She was taking it all in through her tears.

There was a knock on the door. My partner was letting me know that Consuelo's family was in the reception area.

"I'm going to tell them you're trying on some clothes and that you would like to model for them. Is that okay with you?"

She laughed nervously and nodded her head, "Yes, I will do that for them!"

I stepped out and told the family that Consuelo was feeling a bit anxious but that she wanted to give them a fashion show. They were understanding and eager to be supportive of her when she came out.

When I went back into the room, she asked what they had said.

"They're excited and waiting for you. Let's go!"

"Please, Pati, come with me," she asked sweetly.

"Are you kidding me! Of course I'm going to come with you! I wouldn't miss this for anything!" I encouraged her to walk with confidence and smile.

Upon entering the reception area, Consuelo lowered her eyes and began to fidget with her shirt. She was nervous.

At that moment, her son stood up, like the man he was, and walked toward her. "Mami, you look beautiful. Do you like it?"

She took his arm for both physical and emotional support and smiled at him. "Yes, son, I like it very much."

Everyone else rallied around and gave their cheers of approval.

After a few minutes, I piped up, "Consuelo, let's go put on another outfit!"

She and I headed back to the fitting room where she took my hand, squeezed it, and said, "Thank you, Pati. I am so happy."

I gave her a big hug and said, "It's entirely my pleasure. I'm so happy for you too!"

She modeled five more outfits, in addition to the two she had already tried on, and declared that she was done! I showed her how to mix and match and how to add accessories to give each piece a different look. She repeated what I was telling her, pointing to each one and showing me how she would do it. It was touching to see her so willing to get it right.

I collected the clothing and was starting to walk out of the fitting room when she asked if it would be possible to wear one of her new outfits home.

"Yes, absolutely! Which one would you like to wear?"

She pointed to the wide-leg denim pants and a somewhat fitted, sparkly, pink-and-white top that ruched at the sides. She had especially liked it because it was forgiving of the pounds she had gained in the last year.

I went to the counter, and her family joined me as I laid out all the items she had selected. They were so happy for Consuelo as they admired all the pieces. It was wonderful to see how loving and supportive they were. Then, one by one, they thanked me. The son and nephew shook my hand, while the daughters disregarded the register boundaries and gave me a hug.

"Thank you for taking such good care of our mother and for being so nice," they all echoed.

I stopped folding Consuelo's clothing and said, "You have no idea what it means for me to assist your mom tonight and to receive your words of appreciation. You are the type of customers that make my job so worthwhile!"

At that moment, Consuelo came out in her outfit. She looked stylish, and the confidence that was slowly brewing deep within her was emanating from her smile. When they saw her, they all cheered for her once again! I realized I was on the "inside" of something very special. This precious family had suffered so much, and now they were rejoicing. I felt privileged to be sharing this moment with them.

I folded the clothing as complete outfits to make it easier for Consuelo to sort them when she got home. I then placed everything in the bags that I had picked up from Mitchell's office earlier in the evening when we had originally met. They were set to go. I walked around the counter to hand them the bags, and the nephew and daughters took them all.

Consuelo approached me and said, "You were like an angel to me tonight, Pati. I will never forget you. God bless you!"

"The feeling is mutual, Consuelo. I will never forget you, either. Take care of yourself and be happy, my friend."

Her son once again shook my hand and said, "My mom felt intimidated coming into this store tonight, but I told her, 'No, we will find someone to help us,' and we did. It was you! Thank you so much."

His words were so sincere that my eyes filled with tears. I wished them a safe journey and thanked them for shopping with me.

As they turned to walk away, the son put his arm around Consuelo's shoulder, and they smiled at one another. I noticed she put her head down, and I could tell she was crying. Her son's arm hugged her shoulder firmly as they walked out of my view. It was a tender sight—the relationship of a mother and son who had shared sorrows and now a moment of sweet joy.

My partners, Cheryl and Hannah, who had witnessed the transaction from start to finish, congratulated me.

Cheryl said, "Wow, just think! If you hadn't gone to get that other customer the bag, you wouldn't have met them!"

Hannah added, "It was like you were the fairy godmother from *Cinderella*!"

I appreciated my partners' encouragement and smiled as I reflected on Hannah's comment.

"Yeah, I was, wasn't I? And you know what, it felt absolutely *wonderful*!"

The entire evening had been storybook perfect. I was ready to clock out and start my weekend!